T0143815

The Voyage
of the Argo

The Voyage of the Argo (The Argonautica)

Apollonius of Rhodes

MINT EDITIONS

This translation of *The Voyage of the Argo* was first published in 1912.

This edition published by Mint Editions 2020.

ISBN 9781513220291 | E-ISBN 9781513272870

Published by Mint Editions®

**MINT
EDITIONS**

minteditionbooks.com

Publishing Director: Jennifer Newens
Design & Production: Rachel Lopez Metzger
Translation: R.C. Seaton
Typesetting: Westchester Publishing Services

The Voyage of the Argo (The Argonautica)

Apollonius of Rhodes

MINT EDITIONS

This translation of *The Voyage of the Argo* was first published in 1912.

This edition published by Mint Editions 2020.

ISBN 9781513220291 | E-ISBN 9781513272870

Published by Mint Editions®

MINT
EDITIONS

minteditionbooks.com

Publishing Director: Jennifer Newens
Design & Production: Rachel Lopez Metzger
Translation: R.C. Seaton
Typesetting: Westchester Publishing Services

CONTENTS

Introduction

Much has been written about the chronology of Alexandrian literature and the famous Library, founded by Ptolemy Soter, but the dates of the chief writers are still matters of conjecture. The birth of Apollonius Rhodius is placed by scholars at various times between 296 and 260 B.C., while the year of his death is equally uncertain. In fact, we have very little information on the subject. There are two "lives" of Apollonius in the Scholia, both derived from an earlier one which is lost. From these we learn that he was of Alexandria by birth,[1] that he lived in the time of the Ptolemies, and was a pupil of Callimachus; that while still a youth he composed and recited in public his *Argonautica*, and that the poem was condemned, in consequence of which he retired to Rhodes; that there he revised his poem, recited it with great applause, and hence called himself a Rhodian. The second "life" adds: "Some say that he returned to Alexandria and again recited his poem with the utmost success, so that he was honoured with the libraries of the Museum and was buried with Callimachus." The last sentence may be interpreted by the notice of Suidas, who informs us that Apollonius was a contemporary of Eratosthenes, Euphorion and Timarchus, in the time of Ptolemy Euergetes, and that he succeeded Eratosthenes in the headship of the Alexandrian Library. Suidas also informs us elsewhere that Aristophanes at the age of sixty-two succeeded Apollonius in this office. Many modern scholars deny the "bibliothecariate" of Apollonius for chronological reasons, and there is considerable difficulty about it. The date of Callimachus' *Hymn to Apollo*, which closes with some lines (105–113) that are admittedly an allusion to Apollonius, may be put with much probability at 248 or 247 B.C. Apollonius must at that date have been at least twenty years old. Eratosthenes died 196–193 B.C. This would make Apollonius seventy-two to seventy-five when he succeeded Eratosthenes. This is not impossible, it is true, but it is difficult. But the difficulty is taken away if we assume with Ritschl that Eratosthenes resigned his office some years before his death, which allows us to put the birth of Apollonius at about 280, and would solve other difficulties. For instance, if the Librarians were buried within the precincts, it would account for the

---

1. "Or of Naucratis," according to Aelian and Athenaeus.

burial of Apollonius next to Callimachus—Eratosthenes being still alive. However that may be, it is rather arbitrary to take away the "bibliothecariate" of Apollonius, which is clearly asserted by Suidas, on account of chronological calculations which are themselves uncertain. Moreover, it is more probable that the words following "some say" in the second "life" are a remnant of the original life than a conjectural addition, because the first "life" is evidently incomplete, nothing being said about the end of Apollonius' career.

The principal event in his life, so far as we know, was the quarrel with his master Callimachus, which was most probably the cause of his condemnation at Alexandria and departure to Rhodes. This quarrel appears to have arisen from differences of literary aims and taste, but, as literary differences often do, degenerated into the bitterest personal strife. There are references to the quarrel in the writings of both. Callimachus attacks Apollonius in the passage at the end of the *Hymn to Apollo*, already mentioned, also probably in some epigrams, but most of all in his *Ibis*, of which we have an imitation, or perhaps nearly a translation, in Ovid's poem of the same name. On the part of Apollonius there is a passage in the third book of the *Argonautica* (11. 927–947) which is of a polemical nature and stands out from the context, and the well-known savage epigram upon Callimachus.[2] Various combinations have been attempted by scholars, notably by Couat, in his *Poésie Alexandrine*, to give a connected account of the quarrel, but we have not *data* sufficient to determine the order of the attacks, and replies, and counter-attacks. The *Ibis* has been thought to mark the termination of the feud on the curious ground that it was impossible for abuse to go further. It was an age when literary men were more inclined to comment on writings of the past than to produce original work. Literature was engaged in taking stock of itself. Homer was, of course, professedly admired by all, but more admired than imitated. Epic poetry was out of fashion and we find many epigrams of this period—some by Callimachus—directed against the "cyclic" poets, by whom were meant at that time those who were always dragging in conventional and commonplace epithets and phrases peculiar to epic poetry. Callimachus was in accordance with the spirit of the age when he proclaimed "a great book" to be "a great evil," and sought to confine poetical activity within the narrowest limits both of subject and space. Theocritus agreed with him, both in

---

2. Anth. Pal. xi. 275.

principle and practice. The chief characteristics of Alexandrianism are well summarized by Professor Robinson Ellis as follows: "Precision in form and metre, refinement in diction, a learning often degenerating into pedantry and obscurity, a resolute avoidance of everything commonplace in subject, sentiment or allusion." These traits are more prominent in Callimachus than in Apollonius, but they are certainly to be seen in the latter. He seems to have written the *Argonautica* out of bravado, to show that he *could* write an epic poem. But the influence of the age was too strong. Instead of the unity of an Epic we have merely a series of episodes, and it is the great beauty and power of one of these episodes that gives the poem its permanent value—the episode of the love of Jason and Medea. This occupies the greater part of the third book. The first and second books are taken up with the history of the voyage to Colchis, while the fourth book describes the return voyage. These portions constitute a metrical guide book, filled no doubt with many pleasing episodes, such as the rape of Hylas, the boxing match between Pollux and Amycus, the account of Cyzicus, the account of the Amazons, the legend of Talos, but there is no unity running through the poem beyond that of the voyage itself.

The Tale of the Argonauts had been told often before in verse and prose, and many authors' names are given in the Scholia to Apollonius, but their works have perished. The best known earlier account that we have is that in Pindar's fourth Pythian ode, from which Apollonius has taken many details. The subject was one for an epic poem, for its unity might have been found in the working out of the expiation due for the crime of Athamas; but this motive is barely mentioned by our author.

As we have it, the motive of the voyage is the command of Pelias to bring back the golden fleece, and this command is based on Pelias' desire to destroy Jason, while the divine aid given to Jason results from the intention of Hera to punish Pelias for his neglect of the honour due to her. The learning of Apollonius is not deep but it is curious; his general sentiments are not according to the Alexandrian standard, for they are simple and obvious. In the mass of material from which he had to choose the difficulty was to know what to omit, and much skill is shewn in fusing into a tolerably harmonious whole conflicting mythological and historical details. He interweaves with his narrative local legends and the founding of cities, accounts of strange customs, descriptions of works of art, such as that of Ganymede and Eros playing with knucklebones,[3] but prosaically calls himself back to the point from these pleasing digressions by such an expression as "but this would take me too far from my song." His business is the straightforward tale and nothing else. The astonishing geography of the fourth book reminds us of the interest of the age in that subject, stimulated no doubt by the researches of Eratosthenes and others.

The language is that of the conventional epic. Apollonius seems to have carefully studied Homeric glosses, and gives many examples of isolated uses, but his choice of words is by no means limited to Homer. He freely avails himself of Alexandrian words and late uses of Homeric words. Among his contemporaries Apollonius suffers from a comparison with Theocritus, who was a little his senior, but he was much admired by Roman writers who derived inspiration from the great classical writers of Greece by way of Alexandria. In fact Alexandria was a useful bridge between Athens and Rome. The *Argonautica* was translated by Varro Atacinus, copied by Ovid and Virgil, and minutely studied by Valerius Flaccus in his poem of the same name. Some of his finest passages have been appropriated and improved upon by Virgil by the divine right of superior genius.[4] The subject of love had been treated in the romantic spirit before the time of Apollonius in writings that have perished, for instance, in those of Antimachus of Colophon, but the *Argonautica* is perhaps the first poem still extant in which the expression of this spirit is developed with elaboration. The Medea of Apollonius is the direct precursor of the Dido of Virgil, and it is the pathos and passion of the fourth book of the Aeneid that keep alive many a passage of Apollonius.

---

3. iii. 117–124.

4. e.g. compare *Aen.* iv. 305 foll, with Ap. Rh. iv. 355 foll., *Aen.* iv. 327–330 with Ap. Rh. i. 897, 898, *Aen.* iv. 522 foll., with Ap. Rh. iii. 744 foll.

Book I

B eginning with thee, O Phoebus, I will recount the famous deeds of men of old, who, at the behest of King Pelias, down through the mouth of Pontus and between the Cyanean rocks, sped well-benched *Argo* in quest of the golden fleece.

Such was the oracle that Pelias heard, that a hateful doom awaited him—to be slain at the prompting of the man whom he should see coming forth from the people with but one sandal. And no long time after, in accordance with that true report, Jason crossed the stream of wintry Anaurus on foot, and saved one sandal from the mire, but the other he left in the depths held back by the flood. And straightway he came to Pelias to share the banquet which the king was offering to his father Poseidon and the rest of the gods, though he paid no honour to Pelasgian Hera. Quickly the king saw him and pondered, and devised for him the toil of a troublous voyage, in order that on the sea or among strangers he might lose his home-return.

The ship, as former bards relate, Argus wrought by the guidance of Athena. But now I will tell the lineage and the names of the heroes, and of the long sea-paths and the deeds they wrought in their wanderings; may the Muses be the inspirers of my song!

First then let us name Orpheus whom once Calliope bare, it is said, wedded to Thracian Oeagrus, near the Pimpleian height. Men say that he by the music of his songs charmed the stubborn rocks upon the mountains and the course of rivers. And the wild oak-trees to this day, tokens of that magic strain, that grow at Zone on the Thracian shore, stand in ordered ranks close together, the same which under the charm of his lyre he led down from Pieria. Such then was Orpheus whom Aeson's son welcomed to share his toils, in obedience to the behest of Cheiron, Orpheus ruler of Bistonian Pieria.

Straightway came Asterion, whom Cometes begat by the waters of eddying Apidanus; he dwelt at Peiresiae near the Phylleian mount, where mighty Apidanus and bright Enipeus join their streams, coming together from afar.

Next to them from Larisa came Polyphemus, son of Eilatus, who aforetime among the mighty Lapithae, when they were arming themselves against the Centaurs, fought in his younger days; now his limbs were grown heavy with age, but his martial spirit still remained, even as of old.

Nor was Iphiclus long left behind in Phylace, the uncle of Aeson's son; for Aeson had wedded his sister Alcimede, daughter of Phylacus: his kinship with her bade him be numbered in the host.

Nor did Admetus, the lord of Pherae rich in sheep, stay behind beneath the peak of the Chalcodonian mount.

Nor at Alope stayed the sons of Hermes, rich in corn-land, well skilled in craftiness, Erytus and Echion, and with them on their departure their kinsman Aethalides went as the third; him near the streams of Amphrysus Eupolemeia bare, the daughter of Myrmidon, from Phthia; the two others were sprung from Antianeira, daughter of Menetes.

From rich Gyrton came Coronus, son of Caeneus, brave, but not braver than his father. For bards relate that Caeneus though still living perished at the hands of the Centaurs, when apart from other chiefs he routed them; and they, rallying against him, could neither bend nor slay him; but unconquered and unflinching he passed beneath the earth, overwhelmed by the downrush of massy pines.

There came too Titaresian Mopsus, whom above all men the son of Leto taught the augury of birds; and Eurydamas the son of Ctimenus; he dwelt at Dolopian Ctimene near the Xynian lake.

Moreover Actor sent his son Menoetius from Opus that he might accompany the chiefs.

Eurytion followed and strong Eribotes, one the son of Teleon, the other of Irus, Actor's son; the son of Teleon renowned Eribotes, and of Irus Eurytion. A third with them was Oileus, peerless in courage and well skilled to attack the flying foe, when they break their ranks.

Now from Euboea came Canthus eager for the quest, whom Canethus son of Abas sent; but he was not destined to return to Cerinthus. For fate had ordained that he and Mopsus, skilled in the seer's art, should wander and perish in the furthest ends of Libya. For no ill is too remote for mortals to incur, seeing that they buried them in Libya, as far from the Colchians as is the space that is seen between the setting and the rising of the sun.

To him Clytius and Iphitus joined themselves, the warders of Oechalia, sons of Eurytus the ruthless, Eurytus, to whom the Far-shooting god gave his bow; but he had no joy of the gift; for of his own choice he strove even with the giver.

After them came the sons of Aeacus, not both together, nor from the same spot; for they settled far from Aegina in exile, when in their folly they had slain their brother Phocus. Telamon dwelt in the Attic island; but Peleus departed and made his home in Phthia.

After them from Cecropia came warlike Butes, son of brave Teleon, and Phalerus of the ashen spear. Alcon his father sent him forth; yet no other sons had he to care for his old age and livelihood. But him, his well-beloved and only son, he sent forth that amid bold heroes he might shine conspicuous. But Theseus, who surpassed all the sons of Erechtheus, an unseen bond kept beneath the land of Taenarus, for he had followed that path with Peirithous; assuredly both would have lightened for all the fulfilment of their toil.

Tiphys, son of Hagnias, left the Siphaean people of the Thespians, well skilled to foretell the rising wave on the broad sea, and well skilled to infer from sun and star the stormy winds and the time for sailing. Tritonian Athena herself urged him to join the band of chiefs, and he came among them a welcome comrade. She herself too fashioned the swift ship; and with her Argus, son of Arestor, wrought it by her counsels. Wherefore it proved the most excellent of all ships that have made trial of the sea with oars.

After them came Phlias from Araethyrea, where he dwelt in affluence by the favour of his father Dionysus, in his home by the springs of Asopus.

From *Argos* came Talaus and Areius, sons of Bias, and mighty Leodocus, all of whom Pero daughter of Neleus bare; on her account the Aeolid Melampus endured sore affliction in the steading of Iphiclus.

Nor do we learn that Heracles of the mighty heart disregarded the eager summons of Aeson's son. But when he heard a report of the heroes' gathering and had readied Lyrceian *Argos* from Arcadia by the road along which he carried the boar alive that fed in the thickets of Lampeia, near the vast Erymanthian swamp, the boar bound with chains he put down from his huge shoulders at the entrance to the market-place of Mycenae; and himself of his own will set out against the purpose of Eurystheus; and with him went Hylas, a brave comrade, in the flower of youth, to bear his arrows and to guard his bow.

Next to him came a scion of the race of divine Danaus, Nauplius. He was the son of Clytonaeus son of Naubolus; Naubolus was son of Lernus; Lernus we know was the son of Proetus son of Nauplius; and once Amymone daughter of Danaus, wedded to Poseidon, bare Nauplius, who surpassed all men in naval skill.

Idmon came last of all them that dwelt at *Argos*, though he had learnt his own fate by augury, he came, that the people might not grudge him fair renown. He was not in truth the son of Abas, but Leto's son himself begat him to be numbered among the illustrious Aeolids; and himself taught him the art of prophecy—to pay heed to birds and to observe the signs of the burning sacrifice.

Moreover Aetolian Leda sent from Sparta strong Polydeuces and Castor, skilled to guide swift-footed steeds; these her dearly-loved sons she bare at one birth in the house of Tyndareus; nor did she forbid their departure; for she had thoughts worthy of the bride of Zeus.

The sons of Aphareus, Lynceus and proud Idas, came from Arene, both exulting in their great strength; and Lynceus too excelled in keenest sight, if the report is true that that hero could easily direct his sight even beneath the earth.

And with them Neleian Periclymenus set out to come, eldest of all the sons of godlike Neleus who were born at Pylos; Poseidon had given him boundless strength and granted him that whatever shape he should crave during the fight, that he should take in the stress of battle.

Moreover from Arcadia came Amphidamas and Cepheus, who inhabited Tegea and the allotment of Apheidas, two sons of Aleus; and Ancaeus followed them as the third, whom his father Lycurgus sent, the brother older than both. But he was left in the city to care for Aleus now growing old, while he gave his son to join his brothers. Ancaeus went clad in the skin of a Maenalian bear, and wielding in his right hand a huge two-edged battleaxe. For his armour his grandsire had hidden in the house's innermost recess, to see if he might by some means still stay his departure.

There came also Augeias, whom fame declared to be the son of Helios; he reigned over the Eleans, glorying in his wealth; and greatly he desired to behold the Colchian land and Aeetes himself the ruler of the Colchians.

Asterius and Amphion, sons of Hyperasius, came from Achaean Pellene, which once Pelles their grandsire founded on the brows of Aegialus.

After them from Taenarus came Euphemus whom, most swift-footed of men, Europe, daughter of mighty Tityos, bare to Poseidon. He was wont to skim the swell of the grey sea, and wetted not his swift feet, but just dipping the tips of his toes was borne on the watery path.

Yea, and two other sons of Poseidon came; one Erginus, who left the citadel of glorious Miletus, the other proud Ancaeus, who left Parthenia, the seat of Imbrasion Hera; both boasted their skill in sea-craft and in war.

After them from Calydon came the son of Oeneus, strong Meleagrus, and Laocoon—Laocoon the brother of Oeneus, though not by the same mother, for a serving-woman bare him; him, now growing old, Oeneus sent to guard his son: thus Meleagrus, still a youth, entered the bold band of heroes. No other had come superior to him, I ween, except Heracles, if for one year more he had tarried and been nurtured among the Aetolians. Yea, and his uncle, well skilled to fight whether with the javelin or hand to hand, Iphiclus son of Thestius, bare him company on his way.

With him came Palaemonius, son of Olenian Lernus, of Lernus by repute, but his birth was from Hephaestus; and so he was crippled in his feet, but his bodily frame and his valour no one would dare to scorn. Wherefore he was numbered among all the chiefs, winning fame for Jason.

From the Phocians came Iphitus sprung from Naubolus son of Ornytus; once he had been his host when Jason went to Pytho to ask for a response concerning his voyage; for there he welcomed him in his own halls.

Next came Zetes and Calais, sons of Boreas, whom once Oreithyia, daughter of Erechtheus, bare to Boreas on the verge of wintry Thrace; thither it was that Thracian Boreas snatched her away from Cecropia as she was whirling in the dance, hard by Ilissus' stream. And, carrying her far off, to the spot that men called the rock of Sarpedon, near the river Erginus, he wrapped her in dark clouds and forced her to his will. There they were making their dusky wings quiver upon their ankles on both sides as they rose, a great wonder to behold, wings that gleamed with golden scales: and round their backs from the top of the head and neck, hither and thither, their dark tresses were being shaken by the wind.

No, nor had Acastus son of mighty Pelias himself any will to stay behind in the palace of his brave sire, nor Argus, helper of the goddess Athena; but they too were ready to be numbered in the host.

So many then were the helpers who assembled to join the son of Aeson. All the chiefs the dwellers thereabout called Minyae, for the most and the bravest avowed that they were sprung from the blood of the daughters of Minyas; thus Jason himself was the son of Alcimede who was born of Clymene the daughter of Minyas.

Now when all things had been made ready by the thralls, all things that fully-equipped ships are furnished withal when men's business leads them to voyage across the sea, then the heroes took their way through the city to the ship where it lay on the strand that men call

Magnesian Pagasae; and a crowd of people hastening rushed together; but the heroes shone like gleaming stars among the clouds; and each man as he saw them speeding along with their armour would say:

"King Zeus, what is the purpose of Pelias? Whither is he driving forth from the Panachaean land so great a host of heroes? On one day they would waste the palace of Aeetes with baleful fire, should he not yield them the fleece of his own goodwill. But the path is not to be shunned, the toil is hard for those who venture."

Thus they spake here and there throughout the city; but the women often raised their hands to the sky in prayer to the immortals to grant a return, their hearts' desire. And one with tears thus lamented to her fellow:

"Wretched Alcimede, evil has come to thee at last though late, thou hast not ended with splendour of life. Aeson too, ill-fated man! Surely better had it been for him, if he were lying beneath the earth enveloped in his shroud, still unconscious of bitter toils. Would that the dark wave, when the maiden Helle perished, had overwhelmed Phrixus too with the ram: but the dire portent even sent forth a human voice, that it might cause to Alcimede sorrows and countless pains hereafter."

Thus the women spake at the departure of the heroes. And now many thralls, men and women, were gathered together, and his mother, smitten with grief for Jason. And a bitter pang seized every woman's heart; and with them groaned the father in baleful old age, lying on his bed, closely wrapped round. But the hero straightway soothed their pain, encouraging them, and bade the thralls take up his weapons for war; and they in silence with downcast looks took them up. And even as the mother had thrown her arms about her son, so she clung, weeping without stint, as a maiden all alone weeps, falling fondly on the neck of her hoary nurse, a maid who has now no others to care for her, but she drags on a weary life under a stepmother, who maltreats her continually with ever fresh insults, and as she weeps, her heart within her is bound fast with misery, nor can she sob forth all the groans that struggle for utterance; so without stint wept Alcimede straining her son in her arms, and in her yearning grief spake as follows:

"Would that on that day when, wretched woman that I am, I heard King Pelias proclaim his evil behest, I had straightway given up my life and forgotten my cares, so that thou thyself, my son, with thine own hands, mightest have buried me; for that was the only wish left me still to be fulfilled by thee, all the other rewards for thy nurture have I long enjoyed. Now I, once so admired among Achaean women, shall be left behind like a bondwoman in my empty halls, pining away, ill-fated one, for love of thee, thee on whose account I had aforetime so much splendour and renown, my only son for whom I loosed my virgin zone first and last. For to me beyond others the goddess Eileithyia grudged abundant offspring. Alas for my folly! Not once, not even in my dreams did I forebode this, that the flight of Phrixus would bring me woe."

Thus with moaning she wept, and her handmaidens, standing by, lamented; but Jason spake gently to her with comforting words:

"Do not, I pray thee, mother, store up bitter sorrows overmuch, for thou wilt not redeem me from evil by tears, but wilt still add grief to grief. For unseen are the woes that the gods mete out to mortals; be strong to endure thy share of them though with grief in thy heart; take courage from the promises of Athena, and from the answers of the gods (for very favourable oracles has Phoebus given), and then from the help of the chieftains. But do thou remain here, quiet among thy handmaids, and be not a bird of ill omen to the ship; and thither my clansmen and thralls will follow me."

He spake, and started forth to leave the house. And as Apollo goes forth from some fragrant shrine to divine Delos or Claros or Pytho or to broad Lycia near the stream of Xanthus, in such beauty moved Jason through the throng of people; and a cry arose as they shouted together. And there met him aged Iphias, priestess of Artemis guardian of the city, and kissed his right hand, but she had not strength to say a word, for all her eagerness, as the crowd rushed on, but she was left there by the wayside, as the old are left by the young, and he passed on and was gone afar.

Now when he had left the well-built streets of the city he came to the beach of Pagasae, where his comrades greeted him as they stayed together near the ship *Argo*. And he stood at the entering in, and they were gathered to meet him. And they perceived Acastus and Argus coming from the city, and they marvelled when they saw them hasting with all speed, despite the will of Pelias. The one, Argus, son of Arestor, had cast round his shoulders the hide of a bull reaching to his feet, with the black hair upon it, the other, a fair mantle of double fold, which his sister Pelopeia had given him. Still Jason forebore from asking them about each point but bade all be seated for an assembly. And there, upon the folded sails and the mast as it lay on the ground, they all took their seats in order. And among them with goodwill spake Aeson's son:

"All the equipment that a ship needs—for all is in due order—lies ready for our departure. Therefore we will make no long delay in our sailing for these things' sake, when the breezes but blow fair. But, friends,—for common to all is our return to Hellas hereafter, and common to all is our path to the land of Aeetes—now therefore with ungrudging heart choose the bravest to be our leader, who shall be careful for everything, to take upon him our quarrels and covenants with strangers."

Thus he spake; and the young heroes turned their eyes towards bold Heracles sitting in their midst, and with one shout they all enjoined upon him to be their leader; but he, from the place where he sat, stretched forth his right hand and said:

"Let no one offer this honour to me. For I will not consent, and I will forbid any other to stand up. Let the hero who brought us together, himself be the leader of the host."

Thus he spake with high thoughts, and they assented, as Heracles bade; and warlike Jason himself rose up, glad at heart, and thus addressed the eager throng:

"If ye entrust your glory to my care, no longer as before let our path be hindered. Now at last let us propitiate Phoebus with sacrifice and straightway prepare a feast. And until my thralls come, the overseers of my steading, whose care it is to choose out oxen from the herd and drive them hither, we will drag down the ship to the sea, and do ye place all the tackling within, and draw lots for the benches for rowing. Meantime let us build upon the beach an altar to Apollo Embasius[5] who by an oracle promised to point out and show me the paths of the sea, if by sacrifice to him I should begin my venture for King Pelias."

He spake, and was the first to turn to the work, and they stood up in obedience to him; and they heaped their garments, one upon the other, on a smooth stone, which the sea did not strike with its waves, but the stormy surge had cleansed it long before. First of all, by the command of Argus, they strongly girded the ship with a rope well twisted within,[6] stretching it tight on each side, in order that the planks might be well compacted by the bolts and might withstand the opposing force of the surge. And they quickly dug a trench as wide as the space the ship

---

5. i.e. God of embarcation.

6. Or, reading, "they strongly girded the ship outside with a well-twisted rope." In either case there is probably no allusion to (ropes for undergirding) which were carried loose and only used in stormy weather.

covered, and at the prow as far into the sea as it would run when drawn down by their hands. And they ever dug deeper in front of the stem, and in the furrow laid polished rollers; and inclined the ship down upon the first rollers, that so she might glide and be borne on by them. And above, on both sides, reversing the oars, they fastened them round the thole-pins, so as to project a cubit's space. And the heroes themselves stood on both sides at the oars in a row, and pushed forward with chest and hand at once. And then Tiphys leapt on board to urge the youths to push at the right moment; and calling on them he shouted loudly; and they at once, leaning with all their strength, with one push started the ship from her place, and strained with their feet, forcing her onward; and Pelian *Argo* followed swiftly; and they on each side shouted as they rushed on. And then the rollers groaned under the sturdy keel as they were chafed, and round them rose up a dark smoke owing to the weight, and she glided into the sea; but the heroes stood there and kept dragging her back as she sped onward. And round the thole-pins they fitted the oars, and in the ship they placed the mast and the well-made sails and the stores.

Now when they had carefully paid heed to everything, first they distributed the benches by lot, two men occupying one seat; but the middle bench they chose for Heracles and Ancaeus apart from the other heroes, Ancaeus who dwelt in Tegea. For them alone they left the middle bench just as it was and not by lot; and with one consent they entrusted Tiphys with guarding the helm of the well-stemmed ship.

Next, piling up shingle near the sea, they raised there an altar on the shore to Apollo, under the name of Actius[7] and Embasius, and quickly spread above it logs of dried olive-wood. Meantime the herdsmen of Aeson's son had driven before them from the herd two steers. These the younger comrades dragged near the altars, and the others brought lustral water and barley meal, and Jason prayed, calling on Apollo the god of his fathers:

"Hear, O King, that dwellest in Pagasae and the city Aesonis, the city called by my father's name, thou who didst promise me, when I sought thy oracle at Pytho, to show the fulfilment and goal of my journey, for thou thyself hast been the cause of my venture; now do thou thyself guide the ship with my comrades safe and sound, thither and back again to Hellas. Then in thy honour hereafter we will lay again on thy altar

---

7. i.e. God of the shore.

the bright offerings of bulls—all of us who return; and other gifts in countless numbers I will bring to Pytho and Ortygia. And now, come, Far-darter, accept this sacrifice at our hands, which first of all we have offered thee for this ship on our embarcation; and grant, O King, that with a prosperous weird I may loose the hawsers, relying on thy counsel, and may the breeze blow softly with which we shall sail over the sea in fair weather."

He spake, and with his prayer cast the barley meal. And they two girded themselves to slay the steers, proud Ancaeus and Heracles. The latter with his club smote one steer mid-head on the brow, and falling in a heap on the spot, it sank to the ground; and Ancaeus struck the broad neck of the other with his axe of bronze, and shore through the mighty sinews; and it fell prone on both its horns. Their comrades quickly severed the victims' throats, and flayed the hides: they sundered the joints and carved the flesh, then cut out the sacred thigh bones, and covering them all together closely with fat burnt them upon cloven wood. And Aeson's son poured out pure libations, and Idmon rejoiced beholding the flame as it gleamed on every side from the sacrifice, and the smoke of it mounting up with good omen in dark spiral columns; and quickly he spake outright the will of Leto's son:

"For you it is the will of heaven and destiny that ye shall return here with the fleece; but meanwhile both going and returning, countless trials await you. But it is my lot, by the hateful decree of a god, to die somewhere afar off on the mainland of Asia. Thus, though I learnt my fate from evil omens even before now, I have left my fatherland to embark on the ship, that so after my embarking fair fame may be left me in my house."

Thus he spake; and the youths hearing the divine utterance rejoiced at their return, but grief seized them for the fate of Idmon. Now at the hour when the sun passes his noon-tide halt and the ploughlands are just being shadowed by the rocks, as the sun slopes towards the evening dusk, at that hour all the heroes spread leaves thickly upon the sand and lay down in rows in front of the hoary surf-line; and near them were spread vast stores of viands and sweet wine, which the cupbearers had drawn off in pitchers; afterwards they told tales one to another in turn, such as youths often tell when at the feast and the bowl they take delightful pastime, and insatiable insolence is far away. But here the son of Aeson, all helpless, was brooding over each event in his mind, like one oppressed with thought. And Idas noted him and assailed him with loud voice:

"Son of Aeson, what is this plan thou art turning over in mind. Speak out thy thought in the midst. Does fear come on and master thee, fear, that confounds cowards? Be witness now my impetuous spear, wherewith in wars I win renown beyond all others (nor does Zeus aid me so much as my own spear), that no woe will be fatal, no venture will be unachieved, while Idas follows, even though a god should oppose thee. Such a helpmeet am I that thou bringest from Arene."

He spake, and holding a brimming goblet in both hands drank off the unmixed sweet wine; and his lips and dark cheeks were drenched with it; and all the heroes clamoured together and Idmon spoke out openly:

"Vain wretch, thou art devising destruction for thyself before the time. Does the pure wine cause thy bold heart to swell in thy breast to thy ruin, and has it set thee on to dishonour the gods? Other words of comfort there are with which a man might encourage his comrade; but thou hast spoken with utter recklessness. Such taunts, the tale goes, did the sons of Aloeus once blurt out against the blessed gods, and thou dost no wise equal them in valour; nevertheless they were both slain by the swift arrows of Leto's son, mighty though they were."

Thus he spake, and Aphareian Idas laughed out, loud and long, and eyeing him askance replied with biting words:

"Come now, tell me this by thy prophetic art, whether for me too the gods will bring to pass such doom as thy father promised for the sons of Aloeus. And bethink thee how thou wilt escape from my hands alive, if thou art caught making a prophecy vain as the idle wind."

Thus in wrath Idas reviled him, and the strife would have gone further had not their comrades and Aeson's son himself with indignant cry restrained the contending chiefs; and Orpheus lifted his lyre in his left hand and made essay to sing.

He sang how the earth, the heaven and the sea, once mingled together in one form, after deadly strife were separated each from other; and how the stars and the moon and the paths of the sun ever keep their fixed place in the sky; and how the mountains rose, and how the resounding rivers with their nymphs came into being and all creeping things. And he sang how first of all Ophion and Eurynome, daughter of Ocean, held the sway of snowy Olympus, and how through strength of arm one yielded his prerogative to Cronos and the other to Rhea, and how they fell into the waves of Ocean; but the other two meanwhile ruled over the blessed Titan-gods, while Zeus, still a child and with the thoughts of a child, dwelt in the Dictaean cave; and the earthborn Cyclopes had not yet armed him with the bolt, with thunder and lightning; for these things give renown to Zeus.

He ended, and stayed his lyre and divine voice. But though he had ceased they still bent forward with eagerness all hushed to quiet, with ears intent on the enchanting strain; such a charm of song had he left behind in their hearts. Not long after they mixed libations in honour of Zeus, with pious rites as is customary, and poured them upon the burning tongues, and bethought them of sleep in the darkness.

Now when gleaming dawn with bright eyes beheld the lofty peaks of Pelion, and the calm headlands were being drenched as the sea was ruffled by the winds, then Tiphys awoke from sleep; and at once he roused his comrades to go on board and make ready the oars. And a strange cry did the harbour of Pagasae utter, yea and Pelian *Argo* herself, urging them to set forth. For in her a beam divine had been laid which Athena had brought from an oak of Dodona and fitted in the middle of the stem. And the heroes went to the benches one after the other, as they had previously assigned for each to row in his place, and took their seats in due order near their fighting gear. In the middle sat Ancaeus and mighty Heracles, and near him he laid his club, and beneath his tread the ship's keel sank deep. And now the hawsers were being slipped and they poured wine on the sea. But Jason with tears held his eyes away from his fatherland. And just as youths set up a dance in honour of Phoebus either in Pytho or haply in Ortygia, or by the waters of Ismenus, and to the sound of the lyre round his altar all together in time beat the earth with swiftly-moving feet; so they to the sound of Orpheus' lyre smote with their oars the rushing sea-water, and the surge broke over the blades; and on this side and on that the dark brine seethed with foam, boiling terribly through the might of the sturdy heroes. And their arms shone in the sun like flame as the ship sped on; and ever their wake gleamed white far behind, like a path seen over a green plain. On that day all the gods looked down from heaven upon the ship and the might of the heroes, half-divine, the bravest of men then sailing the sea; and on the topmost heights the nymphs of Pelion wondered as they beheld the work of Itonian Athena, and the heroes themselves wielding the oars. And there came down from the mountain-top to the sea Chiron, son of Philyra, and where the white surf broke he dipped his feet, and, often waving with his broad hand, cried out to them at their departure, "Good speed and a sorrowless home-return!" And with him his wife, bearing Peleus' son Achilles on her arm, showed the child to his dear father.

Now when they had left the curving shore of the harbour through the cunning and counsel of prudent Tiphys son of Hagnias, who skilfully handled the well-polished helm that he might guide them steadfastly, then at length they set up the tall mast in the mast-box, and secured it with forestays, drawing them taut on each side, and from it they let down the sail when they had hauled it to the top-mast. And a breeze came down piping shrilly; and upon the deck they fastened the ropes separately round the well-polished pins, and ran quietly past the long Tisaean headland. And for them the son of Oeagrus touched his lyre and sang in rhythmical song of Artemis, saviour of ships, child of a glorious sire, who hath in her keeping those peaks by the sea, and the land of Iolcos; and the fishes came darting through the deep sea, great mixed with small, and followed gambolling along the watery paths. And as when in the track of the shepherd, their master, countless sheep follow to the fold that have fed to the full of grass, and he goes before gaily piping a shepherd's strain on his shrill reed; so these fishes followed; and a chasing breeze ever bore the ship onward.

And straightway the misty land of the Pelasgians, rich in cornfields, sank out of sight, and ever speeding onward they passed the rugged sides of Pelion; and the Sepian headland sank away, and Sciathus appeared in the sea, and far off appeared Piresiae and the calm shore of Magnesia on the mainland and the tomb of Dolops; here then in the evening, as the wind blew against them, they put to land, and paying honour to him at nightfall burnt sheep as victims, while the sea was tossed by the swell: and for two days they lingered on the shore, but on the third day they put forth the ship, spreading on high the broad sail. And even now men call that beach Aphetae[8] of *Argo*.

Thence going forward they ran past Meliboea, escaping a stormy beach and surf-line. And in the morning they saw Homole close at hand leaning on the sea, and skirted it, and not long after they were about to pass by the outfall of the river Amyrus. From there they beheld Eurymenae and the sea-washed ravines of Ossa and Olympus; next they reached the slopes of Pallene, beyond the headland of Canastra, running all night with the wind. And at dawn before them as they journeyed rose Athos, the Thracian mountain, which with its topmost peak overshadows Lemnos, even as far as Myrine, though it lies as far off as the space that a well-trimmed merchantship would traverse up

---

8. i.e. The Starting.

to mid-day. For them on that day, till darkness fell, the breeze blew exceedingly fresh, and the sails of the ship strained to it. But with the setting of the sun the wind left them, and it was by the oars that they reached Lemnos, the Sintian isle.

Here the whole of the men of the people together had been ruthlessly slain through the transgressions of the women in the year gone by. For the men had rejected their lawful wives, loathing them, and had conceived a fierce passion for captive maids whom they themselves brought across the sea from their forays in Thrace; for the terrible wrath of Cypris came upon them, because for a long time they had grudged her the honours due. O hapless women, and insatiate in jealousy to their own ruin! Not their husbands alone with the captives did they slay on account of the marriage-bed, but all the males at the same time, that they might thereafter pay no retribution for the grim murder. And of all the women, Hypsipyle alone spared her aged father Thoas, who was king over the people; and she sent him in a hollow chest to drift over the sea, if haply he should escape. And fishermen dragged him to shore at the island of Oenoe, formerly Oenoe, but afterwards called Sicinus from Sicinus, whom the water-nymph Oenoe bore to Thoas. Now for all the women to tend kine, to don armour of bronze, and to cleave with the plough-share the wheat-bearing fields, was easier than the works of Athena, with which they were busied aforetime. Yet for all that did they often gaze over the broad sea, in grievous fear against the Thracians' coming. So when they saw *Argo* being rowed near the island, straightway crowding in multitude from the gates of Myrine and clad in their harness of war, they poured forth to the beach like ravening Thyiades; for they deemed that the Thracians were come; and with them Hypsipyle, daughter of Thoas, donned her father's harness. And they streamed down speechless with dismay; such fear was wafted about them.

Meantime from the ship the chiefs had sent Aethalides the swift herald, to whose care they entrusted their messages and the wand of Hermes, his sire, who had granted him a memory of all things, that never grew dim; and not even now, though he has entered the unspeakable whirlpools of Acheron, has forgetfulness swept over his soul, but its fixed doom is to be ever changing its abode; at one time to be numbered among the dwellers beneath the earth, at another to be in the light of the sun among living men. But why need I tell at length tales of Aethalides? He at that time persuaded Hypsipyle to receive the new-comers as the day was waning into darkness; nor yet at dawn did they loose the ship's hawsers to the breath of the north wind.

Now the Lemnian women fared through the city and sat down to the assembly, for Hypsipyle herself had so bidden. And when they were all gathered together in one great throng straightway she spake among them with stirring words:

"O friends, come let us grant these men gifts to their hearts' desire, such as it is fitting that they should take on ship-board, food and sweet wine, in order that they may steadfastly remain outside our towers, and may not, passing among us for need's sake, get to know us all too well, and so an evil report be widely spread; for we have wrought a terrible deed and in nowise will it be to their liking, should they learn it. Such is our counsel now, but if any of you can devise a better plan let her rise, for it was on this account that I summoned you hither."

Thus she spake and sat upon her father's seat of stone, and then rose up her dear nurse Polyxo, for very age halting upon her withered feet, bowed over a staff, and she was eager to address them. Near her were seated four virgins, unwedded, crowned with white hair. And she stood in the midst of the assembly and from her bent back she feebly raised her neck and spake thus:

"Gifts, as Hypsipyle herself wishes, let us send to the strangers, for it is better to give them. But for you what device have ye to get profit of your life if the Thracian host fall upon us, or some other foe, as often happens among men, even as now this company is come unforeseen? But if one of the blessed gods should turn this aside yet countless other woes worse than battle, remain behind, when the aged women die off and ye younger ones, without children, reach hateful old age. How then will ye live, hapless ones? Will your oxen of their own accord yoke themselves for the deep ploughlands and draw the earth-cleaving share through the fallow, and forthwith, as the year comes round, reap the harvest? Assuredly, though the fates till now have shunned me in horror, I deem that in the coming year I shall put on the garment of earth, when I have received my meed of burial even so as is right, before the evil days draw near. But I bid you who are younger give good heed to this. For now at your feet a way of escape lies open, if ye trust to the strangers the care of your homes and all your stock and your glorious city."

Thus she spake, and the assembly was filled with clamour. For the word pleased them. And after her straightway Hypsipyle rose up again, and thus spake in reply.

"If this purpose please you all, now will I even send a messenger to the ship."

She spake and addressed Iphinoe close at hand: "Go, Iphinoe, and beg yonder man, whoever it is that leads this array, to come to our land that I may tell him a word that pleases the heart of my people, and bid the men themselves, if they wish, boldly enter the land and the city with friendly intent."

She spake, and dismissed the assembly, and thereafter started to return home. And so Iphinoe came to the Minyae; and they asked with what intent she had come among them. And quickly she addressed her questioners with all speed in these words:

"The maiden Hypsipyle daughter of Thoas, sent me on my way here to you, to summon the captain of your ship, whoever he be, that she may tell him a word that pleases the heart of the people, and she bids yourselves, if ye wish it, straightway enter the land and the city with friendly intent."

Thus she spake and the speech of good omen pleased all. And they deemed that Thoas was dead and that his beloved daughter Hypsipyle was queen, and quickly they sent Jason on his way and themselves made ready to go.

Now he had buckled round his shoulders a purple mantle of double fold, the work of the Tritonian goddess, which Pallas had given him when she first laid the keel-props of the ship *Argo* and taught him how to measure timbers with the rule. More easily wouldst thou cast thy eyes upon the sun at its rising than behold that blazing splendour. For indeed in the middle the fashion thereof was red, but at the ends it was all purple, and on each margin many separate devices had been skilfully inwoven.

In it were the Cyclops seated at their imperishable work, forging a thunderbolt for King Zeus; by now it was almost finished in its brightness and still it wanted but one ray, which they were beating out with their iron hammers as it spurted forth a breath of raging flame.

In it too were the twin sons of Antiope, daughter of Asopus, Amphion and Zethus, and Thebe still ungirt with towers was lying near, whose foundations they were just then laying in eager haste. Zethus on his shoulders was lifting the peak of a steep mountain, like a man toiling hard, and Amphion after him, singing loud and clear on his golden lyre, moved on, and a rock twice as large followed his footsteps.

Next in order had been wrought Cytherea with drooping tresses, wielding the swift shield of Ares; and from her shoulder to her left arm the fastening of her tunic was loosed beneath her breast; and opposite in the shield of bronze her image appeared clear to view as she stood.

And in it there was a well-wooded pasturage of oxen; and about the oxen the Teleboae and the sons of Electryon were fighting; the one party defending themselves, the others, the Taphian raiders, longing to rob them; and the dewy meadow was drenched with their blood, and the many were overmastering the few herdsmen.

And therein were fashioned two chariots, racing, and the one in front Pelops was guiding, as he shook the reins, and with him was Hippodameia at his side, and in pursuit Myrtilus urged his steeds, and with him Oenomaus had grasped his couched spear, but fell as the axle swerved and broke in the nave, while he was eager to pierce the back of Pelops.

And in it was wrought Phoebus Apollo, a stripling not yet grown up, in the act of shooting at mighty Tityos who was boldly dragging his mother by her veil, Tityos whom glorious Elare bare, but Earth nursed him and gave him second birth.

And in it was Phrixus the Minyan as though he were in very deed listening to the ram, while it was like one speaking. Beholding them thou wouldst be silent and wouldst cheat thy soul with the hope of hearing some wise speech from them, and long wouldst thou gaze with that hope.

Such then were the gifts of the Tritonian goddess Athena. And in his right hand Jason held a far-darting spear, which Atalanta gave him once as a gift of hospitality in Maenalus as she met him gladly; for she eagerly desired to follow on that quest; but he himself of his own accord prevented the maid, for he feared bitter strife on account of her love.

And he went on his way to the city like to a bright star, which maidens, pent up in new-built chambers, behold as it rises above their homes, and through the dark air it charms their eyes with its fair red gleam and the maid rejoices, love-sick for the youth who is far away amid strangers, for whom her parents are keeping her to be his bride; like to that star the hero trod the way to the city. And when they had passed within the gates and the city, the women of the people surged behind them, delighting in the stranger, but he with his eyes fixed on the ground fared straight on, till he reached the glorious palace of Hypsipyle; and when he appeared the maids opened the folding doors, fitted with well-fashioned panels. Here Iphinoe leading him quickly through a fair porch set him upon a shining seat opposite her mistress, but Hypsipyle turned her eyes aside and a blush covered her maiden cheeks, yet for all her modesty she addressed him with crafty words:

"Stranger, why stay ye so long outside our towers? for the city is not inhabited by the men, but they, as sojourners, plough the wheat-bearing fields of the Thracian mainland. And I will tell out truly all our evil plight, that ye yourselves too may know it well. When my father Thoas reigned over the citizens, then our folk starting from their homes used to plunder from their ships the dwellings of the Thracians who live opposite, and they brought back hither measureless booty and maidens too. But the counsel of the baneful goddess Cypris was working out its accomplishment, who brought upon them soul destroying infatuation. For they hated their lawful wives, and, yielding to their own mad folly, drove them from their homes; and they took to their beds the captives of their spear, cruel ones. Long in truth we endured it, if haply again, though late, they might change their purpose, but ever the bitter woe grew, twofold. And the lawful children were being dishonoured in their halls, and a bastard race was rising. And thus unmarried maidens and widowed mothers too wandered uncared for through the city; no father heeded his daughter ever so little even though he should see her done to death before his eyes at the hands of an insolent step-dame, nor did sons, as before, defend their mother against unseemly outrage; nor did brothers care at heart for their sister. But in their homes, in the dance, in the assembly and the banquet all their thought was only for their captive maidens; until some god put desperate courage in our hearts no more to receive our lords on their return from Thrace within our towers so that they might either heed the right or might depart and begone elsewhither, they and their captives. So they begged of us all the male children that were left in the city and went back to where even now they dwell on the snowy tilths of Thrace. Do ye therefore stay and settle with us; and shouldst them desire to dwell here, and this finds favour with thee, assuredly thou shalt have the prerogative of my father Thoas; and I deem that thou wilt not scorn our land at all; for it is deep-soiled beyond all other islands that lie in the Aegaean sea. But come now, return to the ship and relate my words to thy comrades, and stay not outside our city."

She spoke, glozing over the murder that had been wrought upon the men; and Jason addressed her in answer:

"Hypsipyle, very dear to our hearts is the help we shall meet with, which thou grantest to us who need thee. And I will return again to the city when I have told everything in order due. But let the sovereignty of the island be thine; it is not in scorn I yield it up, but grievous trials urge me on."

He spake, and touched her right hand; and quickly he turned to go back: and round him the young maids on every side danced in countless numbers in their joy till he passed through the gates. And then they came to the shore in smooth-running wains, bearing with them many gifts, when now he had related from beginning to end the speech which Hypsipyle had spoken when she summoned them; and the maids readily led the men back to their homes for entertainment. For Cypris stirred in them a sweet desire, for the sake of Hephaestus of many counsels, in order that Lemnos might be again inhabited by men and not be ruined.

Thereupon Aeson's son started to go to the royal home of Hypsipyle; and the rest went each his way as chance took them, all but Heracles; for he of his own will was left behind by the ship and a few chosen comrades with him. And straightway the city rejoiced with dances and banquets, being filled with the steam of sacrifice; and above all the immortals they propitiated with songs and sacrifices the illustrious son of Hera and Cypris herself. And the sailing was ever delayed from one day to another; and long would they have lingered there, had not Heracles, gathering together his comrades apart from the women, thus addressed them with reproachful words:

"Wretched men, does the murder of kindred keep us from our native land? Or is it in want of marriage that we have come hither from thence, in scorn of our countrywomen? Does it please us to dwell here and plough the rich soil of Lemnos? No fair renown shall we win by thus tarrying so long with stranger women; nor will some god seize and give us at our prayer a fleece that moves of itself. Let us then return each to his own; but him leave ye to rest all day long in the embrace of Hypsipyle until he has peopled Lemnos with men-children, and so there come to him great glory."

Thus did he chide the band; but no one dared to meet his eye or to utter a word in answer. But just as they were in the assembly they made ready their departure in all haste, and the women came running towards them, when they knew their intent. And as when bees hum round fair lilies pouring forth from their hive in the rock, and all around the dewy meadow rejoices, and they gather the sweet fruit, flitting from one to another; even so the women eagerly poured forth, clustering round the men with loud lament, and greeted each one with hands and voice, praying the blessed gods to grant him a safe return. And so Hypsipyle too prayed, seizing the hands of Aeson's son, and her tears flowed for the loss of her lover:

"Go, and may heaven bring thee back again with thy comrades unharmed, bearing to the king the golden fleece, even as thou wilt and thy heart desireth; and this island and my father's sceptre will be awaiting thee, if on thy return hereafter thou shouldst choose to come hither again; and easily couldst thou gather a countless host of men from other cities. But thou wilt not have this desire, nor do I myself forbode that so it will be. Still remember Hypsipyle when thou art far away and when thou hast returned; and leave me some word of bidding, which I will gladly accomplish, if haply heaven shall grant me to be a mother."

And Aeson's son in admiration thus replied: "Hypsipyle, so may all these things prove propitious by the favour of the blessed gods. But do thou hold a nobler thought of me, since by the grace of Pelias it is enough for me to dwell in my native land; may the gods only release me from my toils. But if it is not my destiny to sail afar and return to the land of Hellas, and if thou shouldst bear a male child, send him when grown up to Pelasgian Iolcus, to heal the grief of my father and mother if so be that he find them still living, in order that, far away from the king, they may be cared for by their own hearth in their home."

He spake, and mounted the ship first of all; and so the rest of the chiefs followed, and, sitting in order, seized the oars; and Argus loosed for them the hawsers from under the sea-beaten rock. Whereupon they mightily smote the water with their long oars, and in the evening by the injunctions of Orpheus they touched at the island of Electra,[9] daughter of Atlas, in order that by gentle initiation they might learn the rites that may not be uttered, and so with greater safety sail over the chilling sea. Of these I will make no further mention; but I bid farewell to the island itself and the indwelling deities, to whom belong those mysteries, which it is not lawful for me to sing.

Thence did they row with eagerness over the depths of the black Sea, having on the one side the land of the Thracians, on the other Imbros on the south; and as the sun was just setting they reached the foreland of the Chersonesus. There a strong south wind blew for them; and raising the sails to the breeze they entered the swift stream of the

---

9. Samothrace.

maiden daughter of Athamas; and at dawn the sea to the north was left behind and at night they were coasting inside the Rhoeteian shore, with the land of Ida on their right. And leaving Dardania they directed their course to Abydus, and after it they sailed past Percote and the sandy beach of Abarnis and divine Pityeia. And in that night, as the ship sped on by sail and oar, they passed right through the Hellespont dark-gleaming with eddies.

There is a lofty island inside the Propontis, a short distance from the Phrygian mainland with its rich cornfields, sloping to the sea, where an isthmus in front of the mainland is flooded by the waves, so low does it lie. And the isthmus has double shores, and they lie beyond the river Aesepus, and the inhabitants round about call the island the Mount of Bears. And insolent and fierce men dwell there, Earthborn, a great marvel to the neighbours to behold; for each one has six mighty hands to lift up, two from his sturdy shoulders, and four below, fitting close to his terrible sides. And about the isthmus and the plain the Doliones had their dwelling, and over them Cyzicus son of Aeneus was king, whom Aenete the daughter of goodly Eusorus bare. But these men the Earthborn monsters, fearful though they were, in nowise harried, owing to the protection of Poseidon; for from him had the Doliones first sprung. Thither *Argo* pressed on, driven by the winds of Thrace, and the Fair haven received her as she sped. There they cast away their small anchorstone by the advice of Tiphys and left it beneath a fountain, the fountain of Artacie; and they took another meet for their purpose, a heavy one; but the first, according to the oracle of the Far-Darter, the Ionians, sons of Neleus, in after days laid to be a sacred stone, as was right, in the temple of Jasonian Athena.

Now the Doliones and Cyzicus himself all came together to meet them with friendliness, and when they knew of the quest and their lineage welcomed them with hospitality, and persuaded them to row further and to fasten their ship's hawsers at the city harbour. Here they built an altar to Ecbasian[10] Apollo and set it up on the beach, and gave heed to sacrifices. And the king of his own bounty gave them sweet wine and sheep in their need; for he had heard a report that whenever a godlike band of heroes should come, straightway he should meet it with gentle words and should have no thought of war. As with Jason, the soft down was just blooming on his chin, nor yet had it been his lot

---

10. i.e. god of disembarcation.

to rejoice in children, but still in his palace his wife was untouched by the pangs of child-birth, the daughter of Percosian Merops, fair-haired Cleite, whom lately by priceless gifts he had brought from her father's home from the mainland opposite. But even so he left his chamber and bridal bed and prepared a banquet among the strangers, casting all fears from his heart. And they questioned one another in turn. Of them would he learn the end of their voyage and the injunctions of Pelias; while they enquired about the cities of the people round and all the gulf of the wide Propontis; but further he could not tell them for all their desire to learn. In the morning they climbed mighty Dindymum that they might themselves behold the various paths of that sea; and they brought their ship from its former anchorage to the harbour, Chytus; and the path they trod is named the path of Jason.

But the Earthborn men on the other side rushed down from the mountain and with crags below blocked up the mouth of vast Chytus towards the sea, like men lying in wait for a wild beast within. But there Heracles had been left behind with the younger heroes and he quickly bent his back-springing bow against the monsters and brought them to earth one after another; and they in their turn raised huge ragged rocks and hurled them. For these dread monsters too, I ween, the goddess Hera, bride of Zeus, had nurtured to be a trial for Heracles. And therewithal came the rest of the martial heroes returning to meet the foe before they reached the height of outlook, and they fell to the slaughter of the Earthborn, receiving them with arrows and spears until they slew them all as they rushed fiercely to battle. And as when woodcutters cast in rows upon the beach long trees just hewn down by their axes, in order that, once sodden with brine, they may receive the strong bolts; so these monsters at the entrance of the foam-fringed harbour lay stretched one after another, some in heaps bending their heads and breasts into the salt waves with their limbs spread out above on the land; others again were resting their heads on the sand of the shore and their feet in the deep water, both alike a prey to birds and fishes at once.

But the heroes, when the contest was ended without fear, loosed the ship's hawsers to the breath of the wind and pressed on through the sea-swell. And the ship sped on under sail all day; but when night came the rushing wind did not hold steadfast, but contrary blasts caught them and held them back till they again approached the hospitable Doliones. And they stepped ashore that same night; and the rock is still called the Sacred Rock round which they threw the ship's hawsers in their haste. Nor did anyone note with care that it was the same island; nor in the night did the Doliones clearly perceive that the heroes were returning; but they deemed that Pelasgian war-men of the Macrians had landed. Therefore they donned their armour and raised their hands against them. And with clashing of ashen spears and shields they fell on each other, like the swift rush of fire which falls on dry brushwood and rears its crest; and the din of battle, terrible and furious, fell upon the people of the Doliones. Nor was the king to escape his fate and return home from battle to his bridal chamber and bed. But Aeson's son leapt upon him as he turned to face him, and smote him in the middle of the breast, and the bone was shattered round the spear; he rolled forward in the sand and filled up the measure of his fate. For that no mortal may escape; but on every side a wide snare encompasses us. And so, when he thought that he had escaped bitter death from the chiefs, fate entangled him that very night in her toils while battling with them; and many champions withal were slain; Heracles killed Telecles and Megabrontes, and Acastus slew Sphodris; and Peleus slew Zelus and Gephyrus swift in war. Telamon of the strong spear slew Basileus. And Idas slew Promeus, and Clytius Hyacinthus, and the two sons of Tyndareus slew Megalossaces and Phlogius. And after them the son of Oeneus slew bold Itomeneus, and Artaceus, leader of men; all of whom the inhabitants still honour with the worship due to heroes. And the rest gave way and fled in terror just as doves fly in terror before swift-winged hawks. And with a din they rushed in a body to the gates; and quickly the city was filled with loud cries at the turning of the dolorous fight. But at dawn both sides perceived the fatal and cureless error; and bitter grief seized the Minyan heroes when they saw before them Cyzicus son of Aeneus fallen in the midst of dust and blood. And for three whole days they lamented and rent their hair, they and the Doliones. Then three times round his tomb they paced in armour of bronze and performed funeral rites and celebrated games, as was meet, upon the meadow-plain, where even now rises the mound of his grave to be seen by men of a later day. No, nor was his bride Cleite left behind her dead husband, but to crown the ill she wrought an ill yet more awful, when she clasped a noose round her neck. Her death even the nymphs of the grove bewailed; and of all the tears for her that they shed to earth from their eyes the goddesses made a fountain, which they call Cleite,[11]

---

11. Cleite means illustrious.

the illustrious name of the hapless maid. Most terrible came that day from Zeus upon the Doliones, women and men; for no one of them dared even to taste food, nor for a long time by reason of grief did they take thought for the toil of the cornmill, but they dragged on their lives eating their food as it was, untouched by fire. Here even now, when the Ionians that dwell in Cyzicus pour their yearly libations for the dead, they ever grind the meal for the sacrificial cakes at the common mill.[12]

After this, fierce tempests arose for twelve days and nights together and kept them there from sailing. But in the next night the rest of the chieftains, overcome by sleep, were resting during the latest period of the night, while Acastus and Mopsus the son of Ampycus kept guard over their deep slumbers. And above the golden head of Aeson's son there hovered a halcyon prophesying with shrill voice the ceasing of the stormy winds; and Mopsus heard and understood the cry of the bird of the shore, fraught with good omen. And some god made it turn aside, and flying aloft it settled upon the stern-ornament of the ship. And the seer touched Jason as he lay wrapped in soft sheepskins and woke him at once, and thus spake:

"Son of Aeson, thou must climb to this temple on rugged Dindymum and propitiate the mother[13] of all the blessed gods on her fair throne, and the stormy blasts shall cease. For such was the voice I heard but now from the halcyon, bird of the sea, which, as as it flew above thee in thy slumber, told me all. For by her power the winds and the sea and all the earth below and the snowy seat of Olympus are complete; and to her, when from the mountains she ascends the mighty heaven, Zeus himself, the son of Cronos, gives place. In like manner the rest of the immortal blessed ones reverence the dread goddess."

Thus he spake, and his words were welcome to Jason's ear. And he arose from his bed with joy and woke all his comrades hurriedly and told them the prophecy of Mopsus the son of Ampycus. And quickly the younger men drove oxen from their stalls and began to lead them to the mountain's lofty summit. And they loosed the hawsers from the sacred rock and rowed to the Thracian harbour; and the heroes climbed the mountain, leaving a few of their comrades in the ship. And to them the Macrian heights and all the coast of Thrace opposite appeared to view close at hand. And there appeared the misty mouth of Bosporus

---

12. i.e. to avoid grinding it at home.
13. Rhea.

APOLLONIUS OF RHODES

and the Mysian hills; and on the other side the stream of the river Aesepus and the city and Nepeian plain of Adrasteia. Now there was a sturdy stump of vine that grew in the forest, a tree exceeding old; this they cut down, to be the sacred image of the mountain goddess; and Argus smoothed it skilfully, and they set it upon that rugged hill beneath a canopy of lofty oaks, which of all trees have their roots deepest. And near it they heaped an altar of small stones, and wreathed their brows with oak leaves and paid heed to sacrifice, invoking the mother of Dindymum, most venerable, dweller in Phrygia, and Titias and Cyllenus, who alone of many are called dispensers of doom and assessors of the Idaean mother,—the Idaean Dactyls of Crete, whom once the nymph Anchiale, as she grasped with both hands the land of Oaxus, bare in the Dictaean cave. And with many prayers did Aeson's son beseech the goddess to turn aside the stormy blasts as he poured libations on the blazing sacrifice; and at the same time by command of Orpheus the youths trod a measure dancing in full armour, and clashed with their swords on their shields, so that the ill-omened cry might be lost in the air—the wail which the people were still sending up in grief for their king. Hence from that time forward the Phrygians propitiate Rhea with the wheel and the drum. And the gracious goddess, I ween, inclined her heart to pious sacrifices; and favourable signs appeared. The trees shed abundant fruit, and round their feet the earth of its own accord put forth flowers from the tender grass. And the beasts of the wild wood left their lairs and thickets and came up fawning on them with their tails. And she caused yet another marvel; for hitherto there was no flow of water on Dindymum, but then for them an unceasing stream gushed forth from the thirsty peak just as it was, and the dwellers around in after times called that stream, the spring of Jason. And then they made a feast in honour of the goddess on the Mount of Bears, singing the praises of Rhea most venerable; but at dawn the winds had ceased and they rowed away from the island.

Thereupon a spirit of contention stirred each chieftain, who should be the last to leave his oar. For all around the windless air smoothed the swirling waves and lulled the sea to rest. And they, trusting in the calm, mightily drove the ship forward; and as she sped through the salt sea, not even the storm-footed steeds of Poseidon would have overtaken her. Nevertheless when the sea was stirred by violent blasts which were just rising from the rivers about evening, forspent with toil, they ceased. But Heracles by the might of his arms pulled the weary rowers along all together, and made the strong-knit timbers of the ship to quiver. But when, eager to reach the Mysian mainland, they passed along in sight of the mouth of Rhyndacus and the great cairn of Aegaeon, a little way from Phrygia, then Heracles, as he ploughed up the furrows of the roughened surge, broke his oar in the middle. And one half he held in both his hands as he fell sideways, the other the sea swept away with its receding wave. And he sat up in silence glaring round; for his hands were unaccustomed to lie idle.

Now at the hour when from the field some delver or ploughman goes gladly home to his hut, longing for his evening meal, and there on the threshold, all squalid with dust, bows his wearied knees, and, beholding his hands worn with toil, with many a curse reviles his belly; at that hour the heroes reached the homes of the Cianian land near the Arganthonian mount and the outfall of Cius. Them as they came in friendliness, the Mysians, inhabitants of that land, hospitably welcomed, and gave them in their need provisions and sheep and abundant wine. Hereupon some brought dried wood, others from the meadows leaves for beds which they gathered in abundance for strewing, whilst others were twirling sticks to get fire; others again were mixing wine in the bowl and making ready the feast, after sacrificing at nightfall to Apollo Ecbasius.

But the son of Zeus having duly enjoined on his comrades to prepare the feast took his way into a wood, that he might first fashion for himself an oar to fit his hand. Wandering about he found a pine not burdened with many branches, nor too full of leaves, but like to the shaft of a tall poplar; so great was it both in length and thickness to look at. And quickly he laid on the ground his arrow-holding quiver together with his bow, and took off his lion's skin. And he loosened the pine from the ground with his bronze-tipped club and grasped the trunk with both hands at the bottom, relying on his strength; and he pressed it against his broad shoulder with legs wide apart; and clinging close he raised it from the ground deep-rooted though it was, together with clods of earth. And as when unexpectedly, just at the time of the stormy setting of baleful Orion, a swift gust of wind strikes down from above, and wrenches a ship's mast from its stays, wedges and all; so did Heracles lift the pine. And at the same time he took up his bow and arrows, his lion skin and club, and started on his return.

Meantime Hylas with pitcher of bronze in hand had gone apart from the throng, seeking the sacred flow of a fountain, that he might be quick in drawing water for the evening meal and actively make all things ready in due order against his lord's return. For in such ways did Heracles nurture him from his first childhood when he had carried him off from the house of his father, goodly Theiodamas, whom the hero pitilessly slew among the Dryopians because he withstood him about an ox for the plough. Theiodamas was cleaving with his plough the soil of fallow land when he was smitten with the curse; and Heracles bade him give up the ploughing ox against his will. For he desired to find some pretext for war against the Dryopians for their bane, since they dwelt there reckless of right. But these tales would lead me far astray from my song. And quickly Hylas came to the spring which the people who dwell thereabouts call Pegae. And the dances of the nymphs were just now being held there; for it was the care of all the nymphs that haunted that lovely headland ever to hymn Artemis in songs by night. All who held the mountain peaks or glens, all they were ranged far off guarding the woods; but one, a water-nymph was just rising from the fair-flowing spring; and the boy she perceived close at hand with the rosy flush of his beauty and sweet grace. For the full moon beaming from the sky smote him. And Cypris made her heart faint, and in her confusion she could scarcely gather her spirit back to her. But as soon as he dipped the pitcher in the stream, leaning to one side, and the brimming water rang loud as it poured against the sounding bronze, straightway she laid her left arm above upon his neck yearning to kiss his tender mouth; and with her right hand she drew down his elbow, and plunged him into the midst of the eddy.

Alone of his comrades the hero Polyphemus, son of Eilatus, as he went forward on the path, heard the boy's cry, for he expected the return of mighty Heracles. And he rushed after the cry, near Pegae, like some beast of the wild wood whom the bleating of sheep has reached from afar, and burning with hunger he follows, but does not fall in with the flocks; for the shepherds beforehand have penned them in the fold, but he groans and roars vehemently until he is weary. Thus vehemently at that time did the son of Eilatus groan and wandered shouting round the spot; and his voice rang piteous. Then quickly drawing his great sword he started in pursuit, in fear lest the boy should be the prey of wild beasts, or men should have lain in ambush for him faring all alone, and be carrying him off, an easy prey. Hereupon as he brandished his bare sword in his hand he met Heracles himself on the path, and well he knew him as he hastened to the ship through the darkness. And straightway he told the wretched calamity while his heart laboured with his panting breath.

"My poor friend, I shall be the first to bring thee tidings of bitter woe. Hylas has gone to the well and has not returned safe, but robbers have attacked and are carrying him off, or beasts are tearing him to pieces; I heard his cry."

Thus he spake; and when Heracles heard his words, sweat in abundance poured down from his temples and the black blood boiled beneath his heart. And in wrath he hurled the pine to the ground and hurried along the path whither his feet bore on his impetuous soul. And as when a bull stung by a gadfly tears along, leaving the meadows and the marsh land, and recks not of herdsmen or herd, but presses on, now without check, now standing still, and raising his broad neck he bellows loudly, stung by the maddening fly; so he in his frenzy now would ply his swift knees unresting, now again would cease from toil and shout afar with loud pealing cry.

But straightway the morning star rose above the topmost peaks and the breeze swept down; and quickly did Tiphys urge them to go aboard and avail themselves of the wind. And they embarked eagerly forthwith; and they drew up the ship's anchors and hauled the ropes astern. And the sails were bellied out by the wind, and far from the coast were they joyfully borne past the Posideian headland. But at the hour when gladsome dawn shines from heaven, rising from the east, and the paths stand out clearly, and the dewy plains shine with a bright gleam, then at length they were aware that unwittingly they had abandoned those men. And a fierce quarrel fell upon them, and violent tumult, for that they had sailed and left behind the bravest of their comrades. And Aeson's son, bewildered by their hapless plight, said never a word, good or bad; but sat with his heavy load of grief, eating out his heart. And wrath seized Telamon, and thus he spake:

"Sit there at thy ease, for it was fitting for thee to leave Heracles behind; from thee the project arose, so that his glory throughout Hellas should not overshadow thee, if so be that heaven grants us a return home. But what pleasure is there in words? For I will go, I only, with none of thy comrades, who have helped thee to plan this treachery."

He spake, and rushed upon Tiphys son of Hagnias; and his eyes sparkled like flashes of ravening flame. And they would quickly have turned back to the land of the Mysians, forcing their way through the deep sea and the unceasing blasts of the wind, had not the two sons of

Thracian Boreas held back the son of Aeacus with harsh words. Hapless ones, assuredly a bitter vengeance came upon them thereafter at the hands of Heracles, because they stayed the search for him. For when they were returning from the games over Pelias dead he slew them in sea-girt Tenos and heaped the earth round them, and placed two columns above, one of which, a great marvel for men to see, moves at the breath of the blustering north wind. These things were thus to be accomplished in after times. But to them appeared Glaucus from the depths of the sea, the wise interpreter of divine Nereus, and raising aloft his shaggy head and chest from his waist below, with sturdy hand he seized the ship's keel, and then cried to the eager crew:

"Why against the counsel of mighty Zeus do ye purpose to lead bold Heracles to the city of Aeetes? At *Argos* it is his fate to labour for insolent Eurystheus and to accomplish full twelve toils and dwell with the immortals, if so be that he bring to fulfilment a few more yet; wherefore let there be no vain regret for him. Likewise it is destined for Polyphemus to found a glorious city at the mouth of Cius among the Mysians and to fill up the measure of his fate in the vast land of the Chalybes. But a goddess-nymph through love has made Hylas her husband, on whose account those two wandered and were left behind."

He spake, and with a plunge wrapped him about with the restless wave; and round him the dark water foamed in seething eddies and dashed against the hollow ship as it moved through the sea. And the heroes rejoiced, and Telamon son of Aeacus came in haste to Jason, and grasping his hand in his own embraced him with these words:

"Son of Aeson, be not wroth with me, if in my folly I have erred, for grief wrought upon me to utter a word arrogant and intolerable. But let me give my fault to the winds and let our hearts be joined as before."

Him the son of Aeson with prudence addressed: "Good friend, assuredly with an evil word didst thou revile me, saying before them all that I was the wronger of a kindly man. But not for long will I nurse bitter wrath, though indeed before I was grieved. For it was not for flocks of sheep, no, nor for possessions that thou wast angered to fury, but for a man, thy comrade. And I were fain thou wouldst even champion me against another man if a like thing should ever befall me."

He spake, and they sat down, united as of old. But of those two, by the counsel of Zeus, one, Polyphemus son of Eilatus, was destined to found and build a city among the Mysians bearing the river's name, and the other, Heracles, to return and toil at the labours of Eurystheus. And he threatened to lay waste the Mysian land at once, should they not discover for him the doom of Hylas, whether living or dead. And for him they gave pledges choosing out the noblest sons of the people and took an oath that they would never cease from their labour of search. Therefore to this day the people of Cius enquire for Hylas the son of Theiodamas; and take thought for the well-built Trachis. For there did Heracles settle the youths whom they sent from Cius as pledges.

And all day long and all night the wind bore the ship on, blowing fresh and strong; but when dawn rose there was not even a breath of air. And they marked a beach jutting forth from a bend of the coast, very broad to behold, and by dint of rowing came to land at sunrise.

Book II

H ere were the oxstalls and farm of Amycus, the haughty king of
the Bebrycians, whom once a nymph, Bithynian Melie, united
to Poseidon Genethlius, bare—the most arrogant of men; for even for
strangers he laid down an insulting ordinance, that none should depart
till they had made trial of him in boxing; and he had slain many of the
neighbours. And at that time too he went down to the ship and in his
insolence scorned to ask them the occasion of their voyage, and who
they were, but at once spake out among them all:

"Listen, ye wanderers by sea, to what it befits you to know. It is
the rule that no stranger who comes to the Bebrycians should depart
till he has raised his hands in battle against mine. Wherefore select
your bravest warrior from the host and set him here on the spot to
contend with me in boxing. But if ye pay no heed and trample my
decrees under foot, assuredly to your sorrow will stern necessity come
upon you."

Thus he spake in his pride, but fierce anger seized them when they
heard it, and the challenge smote Polydeuces most of all. And quickly
he stood forth his comrades' champion, and cried:

"Hold now, and display not to us thy brutal violence, whoever thou
art; for we will obey thy rules, as thou sayest. Willingly now do I myself
undertake to meet thee."

Thus he spake outright; but the other with rolling eyes glared on
him, like to a lion struck by a javelin when hunters in the mountains are
hemming him round, and, though pressed by the throng, he recks no
more of them, but keeps his eyes fixed, singling out that man only who
struck him first and slew him not. Hereupon the son of Tyndareus laid
aside his mantle, closely-woven, delicately-wrought, which one of the
Lemnian maidens had given him as a pledge of hospitality; and the king
threw down his dark cloak of double fold with its clasps and the knotted
crook of mountain olive which he carried. Then straightway they looked
and chose close by a spot that pleased them and bade their comrades sit
upon the sand in two lines; nor were they alike to behold in form or in
stature. The one seemed to be a monstrous son of baleful Typhoeus or of
Earth herself, such as she brought forth aforetime, in her wrath against
Zeus; but the other, the son of Tyndareus, was like a star of heaven,
whose beams are fairest as it shines through the nightly sky at eventide.

Such was the son of Zeus, the bloom of the first down still on his cheeks, still with the look of gladness in his eyes. But his might and fury waxed like a wild beast's; and he poised his hands to see if they were pliant as before and were not altogether numbed by toil and rowing. But Amycus on his side made no trial; but standing apart in silence he kept his eyes upon his foe, and his spirit surged within him all eager to dash the life-blood from his breast. And between them Lycoreus, the henchman of Amycus, placed at their feet on each side two pairs of gauntlets made of raw hide, dry, exceeding tough. And the king addressed the hero with arrogant words:

"Whichever of these thou wilt, without casting lots, I grant thee freely, that thou mayst not blame me hereafter. Bind them about thy hands; thou shalt learn and tell another how skilled I am to carve the dry oxhides and to spatter men's cheeks with blood."

Thus he spake; but the other gave back no taunt in answer, but with a light smile readily took up the gauntlets that lay at his feet; and to him came Castor and mighty Talaus, son of Bias, and they quickly bound the gauntlets about his hands, often bidding him be of good courage. And to Amycus came Aretus and Ornytus, but little they knew, poor fools, that they had bound them for the last time on their champion, a victim of evil fate.

Now when they stood apart and were ready with their gauntlets, straightway in front of their faces they raised their heavy hands and matched their might in deadly strife. Hereupon the Bebrycian king—even as a fierce wave of the sea rises in a crest against a swift ship, but she by the skill of the crafty pilot just escapes the shock when the billow is eager to break over the bulwark—so he followed up the son of Tyndareus, trying to daunt him, and gave him no respite. But the hero, ever unwounded, by his skill baffled the rush of his foe, and he quickly noted the brutal play of his fists to see where he was invincible in strength, and where inferior, and stood unceasingly and returned blow for blow. And as when shipwrights with their hammers smite ships' timbers to meet the sharp clamps, fixing layer upon layer; and the blows resound one after another; so cheeks and jaws crashed on both sides, and a huge clattering of teeth arose, nor did they cease ever from striking their blows until laboured gasping overcame both. And standing a little apart they wiped from their foreheads sweat in abundance, wearily panting for breath. Then back they rushed together again, as two bulls fight in furious rivalry for a grazing heifer. Next Amycus rising on tiptoe, like one who slays an ox, sprung to his full height and swung his heavy hand down upon his rival; but the hero swerved aside from the rush, turning his head, and just received the arm on his shoulder; and coming near and slipping his knee past the king's, with a rush he struck him above the ear, and broke the bones inside, and the king in agony fell upon his knees; and the Minyan heroes shouted for joy; and his life was poured forth all at once.

Nor were the Bebrycians reckless of their king; but all together took up rough clubs and spears and rushed straight on Polydeuces. But in front of him stood his comrades, their keen swords drawn from the sheath. First Castor struck upon the head a man as he rushed at him: and it was cleft in twain and fell on each side upon his shoulders. And Polydeuces slew huge Itymoneus and Mimas. The one, with a sudden leap, he smote beneath the breast with his swift foot and threw him in the dust; and as the other drew near he struck him with his right hand above the left eyebrow, and tore away his eyelid and the eyeball was left bare. But Oreides, insolent henchman of Amycus, wounded Talaus son of Bias in the side, but did not slay him, but only grazing the skin the bronze sped under his belt and touched not the flesh. Likewise Aretus with well-seasoned club smote Iphitus, the steadfast son of Eurytus, not yet destined to an evil death; assuredly soon was he himself to be slain by the sword of Clytius. Then Ancaeus, the dauntless son of Lycurgus, quickly seized his huge axe, and in his left hand holding a bear's dark hide, plunged into the midst of the Bebrycians with furious onset; and with him charged the sons of Aeacus, and with them started warlike Jason. And as when amid the folds grey wolves rush down on a winter's day and scare countless sheep, unmarked by the keen-scented dogs and the shepherds too, and they seek what first to attack and carry off, often glaring around, but the sheep are just huddled together and trample on one another; so the heroes grievously scared the arrogant Bebrycians. And as shepherds or beekeepers smoke out a huge swarm of bees in a rock, and they meanwhile, pent up in their hive, murmur with droning hum, till, stupefied by the murky smoke, they fly forth far from the rock; so they stayed steadfast no longer, but scattered themselves inland through Bebrycia, proclaiming the death of Amycus; fools, not to perceive that another woe all unforeseen was hard upon them. For at that hour their vineyards and villages were being ravaged by the hostile spear of Lycus and the Mariandyni, now that their king was gone. For they were ever at strife about the ironbearing land. And now the foe was destroying their steadings and farms, and now the heroes from all sides were driving off their countless sheep, and one spake among his fellows thus:

"Bethink ye what they would have done in their cowardice if haply some god had brought Heracles hither. Assuredly, if he had been here, no trial would there have been of fists, I ween, but when the king drew near to proclaim his rules, the club would have made him forget his pride and the rules to boot. Yea, we left him uncared for on the strand and we sailed oversea; and full well each one of us shall know our baneful folly, now that he is far away."

Thus he spake, but all these things had been wrought by the counsels of Zeus. Then they remained there through the night and tended the hurts of the wounded men, and offered sacrifice to the immortals, and made ready a mighty meal; and sleep fell upon no man beside the bowl and the blazing sacrifice. They wreathed their fair brows with the bay that grew by the shore, whereto their hawsers were bound, and chanted a song to the lyre of Orpheus in sweet harmony; and the windless shore was charmed by their song; and they celebrated the Therapnaean son of Zeus.[14]

But when the sun rising from far lands lighted up the dewy hills and wakened the shepherds, then they loosed their hawsers from the stem of the bay-tree and put on board all the spoil they had need to take; and with a favouring wind they steered through the eddying Bosporus. Hereupon a wave like a steep mountain rose aloft in front as though rushing upon them, ever upheaved above the clouds; nor would you say that they could escape grim death, for in its fury it hangs over the middle of the ship, like a cloud, yet it sinks away into calm if it meets with a skilful helmsman. So they by the steering-craft of Tiphys escaped, unhurt but sore dismayed. And on the next day they fastened the hawsers to the coast opposite the Bithynian land.

There Phineus, son of Agenor, had his home by the sea, Phineus who above all men endured most bitter woes because of the gift of prophecy which Leto's son had granted him aforetime. And he reverenced not a whit even Zeus himself, for he foretold unerringly to men his sacred will. Wherefore Zeus sent upon him a lingering old age, and took from his eyes the pleasant light, and suffered him not to have joy of the dainties

---

14. i.e. Polydeuces.

untold that the dwellers around ever brought to his house, when they came to enquire the will of heaven. But on a sudden, swooping through the clouds, the Harpies with their crooked beaks incessantly snatched the food away from his mouth and hands. And at times not a morsel of food was left, at others but a little, in order that he might live and be tormented. And they poured forth over all a loathsome stench; and no one dared not merely to carry food to his mouth but even to stand at a distance; so foully reeked the remnants of the meal. But straightway when he heard the voice and the tramp of the band he knew that they were the men passing by, at whose coming Zeus' oracle had declared to him that he should have joy of his food. And he rose from his couch, like a lifeless dream, bowed over his staff, and crept to the door on his withered feet, feeling the walls; and as he moved, his limbs trembled for weakness and age; and his parched skin was caked with dirt, and naught but the skin held his bones together. And he came forth from the hall with wearied knees and sat on the threshold of the courtyard; and a dark stupor covered him, and it seemed that the earth reeled round beneath his feet, and he lay in a strengthless trance, speechless. But when they saw him they gathered round and marvelled. And he at last drew laboured breath from the depths of his chest and spoke among them with prophetic utterance:

"Listen, bravest of all the Hellenes, if it be truly ye, whom by a king's ruthless command Jason is leading on the ship *Argo* in quest of the fleece. It is ye truly. Even yet my soul by its divination knows everything. Thanks I render to thee, O king, son of Leto, plunged in bitter affliction though I be. I beseech you by Zeus the god of suppliants, the sternest foe to sinful men, and for the sake of Phoebus and Hera herself, under whose especial care ye have come hither, help me, save an ill-fated man from misery, and depart not uncaring and leaving me thus as ye see. For not only has the Fury set her foot on my eyes and I drag on to the end a weary old age; but besides my other woes a woe hangs over me—the bitterest of all. The Harpies, swooping down from some unseen den of destruction ever snatch the food from my mouth. And I have no device to aid me. But it were easier, when I long for a meal, to escape my own thoughts than them, so swiftly do they fly through the air. But if haply they *do* leave me a morsel of food it reeks of decay and the stench is unendurable, nor could any mortal bear to draw near even for a moment, no, not if his heart were wrought of adamant. But necessity, bitter and insatiate, compels me to abide and abiding to put food in my cursèd belly. These pests, the oracle declares, the sons of Boreas shall restrain. And no strangers are they that shall ward them off if indeed I am Phineus who was once renowned among men for wealth and the gift of prophecy, and if I am the son of my father Agenor; and, when I ruled among the Thracians, by my bridal gifts I brought home their sister Cleopatra to be my wife."

So spake Agenor's son; and deep sorrow seized each of the heroes, and especially the two sons of Boreas. And brushing away a tear they drew nigh, and Zetes spake as follows, taking in his own the hand of the grief-worn sire:

"Unhappy one, none other of men is more wretched than thou, methinks. Why upon thee is laid the burden of so many sorrows? Hast thou with baneful folly sinned against the gods through thy skill in prophecy? For this are they greatly wroth with thee? Yet our spirit is dismayed within us for all our desire to aid thee, if indeed the god has granted this privilege to us two. For plain to discern to men of earth are the reproofs of the immortals. And we will never check the Harpies when they come, for all our desire, until thou hast sworn that for this we shall not lose the favour of heaven."

Thus he spake; and towards him the aged sire opened his sightless eyes, and lifted them up and replied with these words:

"Be silent, store not up such thoughts in thy heart, my child. Let the son of Leto be my witness, he who of his gracious will taught me the lore of prophecy, and be witness the ill-starred doom which possesses me and this dark cloud upon my eyes, and the gods of the underworld— and may their curse be upon me if I die perjured thus—no wrath from heaven will fall upon you two for your help to me."

Then were those two eager to help him because of the oath. And quickly the younger heroes prepared a feast for the aged man, a last prey for the Harpies; and both stood near him, to smite with the sword those pests when they swooped down. Scarcely had the aged man touched the food when they forthwith, like bitter blasts or flashes of lightning, suddenly darted from the clouds, and swooped down with a yell, fiercely craving for food; and the heroes beheld them and shouted in the midst of their onrush; but they at the cry devoured everything and sped away over the sea afar; and an intolerable stench remained. And behind them the two sons of Boreas raising their swords rushed in pursuit. For Zeus imparted to them tireless strength; but without Zeus they could not have followed, for the Harpies used ever to outstrip the blasts of the west wind when they came to Phineus and when they left him. And as when, upon the mountain-side, hounds, cunning in the chase, run in the track of horned goats or deer, and as they strain a little behind gnash their teeth upon the edge of their jaws in vain; so Zetes and Calais rushing very near just grazed the Harpies in vain with their finger-tips. And assuredly they would have torn them to pieces, despite heaven's will, when they had overtaken them far off at the Floating Islands, had not swift Iris seen them and leapt down from the sky from heaven above, and checked them with these words:

"It is not lawful, O sons of Boreas, to strike with your swords the Harpies, the hounds of mighty Zeus; but I myself will give you a pledge, that hereafter they shall not draw near to Phineus."

With these words she took an oath by the waters of Styx, which to all the gods is most dread and most awful, that the Harpies would never thereafter again approach the home of Phineus, son of Agenor, for so it was fated. And the heroes yielding to the oath, turned back their flight to the ship. And on account of this men call them the Islands of Turning though aforetime they called them the Floating Islands. And the Harpies and Iris parted. They entered their den in Minoan Crete; but she sped up to Olympus, soaring aloft on her swift wings.

Meanwhile the chiefs carefully cleansed the old man's squalid skin and with due selection sacrificed sheep which they had borne away from the spoil of Amycus. And when they had laid a huge supper in the hall, they sat down and feasted, and with them feasted Phineus ravenously, delighting his soul, as in a dream. And there, when they had taken their fill of food and drink, they kept awake all night waiting for the sons of Boreas. And the aged sire himself sat in the midst, near the hearth, telling of the end of their voyage and the completion of their journey:

"Listen then. Not everything is it lawful for you to know clearly; but whatever is heaven's will, I will not hide. I was infatuated aforetime, when in my folly I declared the will of Zeus in order and to the end. For he himself wishes to deliver to men the utterances of the prophetic art incomplete, in order that they may still have some need to know the will of heaven.

"First of all, after leaving me, ye will see the twin Cyanean rocks where the two seas meet. No one, I ween, has won his escape between them. For they are not firmly fixed with roots beneath, but constantly clash against one another to one point, and above a huge mass of salt water rises in a crest, boiling up, and loudly dashes upon the hard beach.

Wherefore now obey my counsel, if indeed with prudent mind and reverencing the blessed gods ye pursue your way; and perish not foolishly by a self-sought death, or rush on following the guidance of youth. First entrust the attempt to a dove when ye have sent her forth from the ship. And if she escapes safe with her wings between the rocks to the open sea, then no more do ye refrain from the path, but grip your oars well in your hands and cleave the sea's narrow strait, for the light of safety will be not so much in prayer as in strength of hands. Wherefore let all else go and labour boldly with might and main, but ere then implore the gods as ye will, I forbid you not. But if she flies onward and perishes midway, then do ye turn back; for it is better to yield to the immortals. For ye could not escape an evil doom from the rocks, not even if *Argo* were of iron.

"O hapless ones, dare not to transgress my divine warning, even though ye think that I am thrice as much hated by the sons of heaven as I am, and even more than thrice; dare not to sail further with your ship in despite of the omen. And as these things will fall, so shall they fall. But if ye shun the clashing rocks and come scatheless inside Pontus, straightway keep the land of the Bithynians on your right and sail on, and beware of the breakers, until ye round the swift river Rhebas and the black beach, and reach the harbour of the Isle of Thynias. Thence ye must turn back a little space through the sea and beach your ship on the land of the Mariandyni lying opposite. Here is a downward path to the abode of Hades, and the headland of Acherusia stretches aloft, and eddying Acheron cleaves its way at the bottom, even through the headland, and sends its waters forth from a huge ravine. And near it ye will sail past many hills of the Paphlagonians, over whom at the first Eneteian Pelops reigned, and of his blood they boast themselves to be.

"Now there is a headland opposite Helice the Bear, steep on all sides, and they call it Carambis, about whose crests the blasts of the north wind are sundered. So high in the air does it rise turned towards the sea. And when ye have rounded it broad Aegialus stretches before you; and at the end of broad Aegialus, at a jutting point of coast, the waters of the river Halys pour forth with a terrible roar; and after it Iris flowing near, but smaller in stream, rolls into the sea with white eddies. Onward from thence the bend of a huge and towering cape reaches out from the land, next Thermodon at its mouth flows into a quiet bay at the Themiscyreian headland, after wandering through a broad continent. And here is the plain of Doeas, and near are the three cities of the Amazons, and after them the Chalybes, most wretched of men, possess a soil rugged and unyielding—sons of toil, they busy themselves with working iron. And near them dwell the Tibareni, rich in sheep, beyond the Genetaean headland of Zeus, lord of hospitality. And bordering on it the Mossynoeci next in order inhabit the well-wooded mainland and the parts beneath the mountains, who have built in towers made from trees their wooden homes and well-fitted chambers, which they call Mossynes, and the people themselves take their name from them. After passing them ye must beach your ship upon a smooth island, when ye have driven away with all manner of skill the ravening birds, which in countless numbers haunt the desert island. In it the Queens of the Amazons, Otrere and Antiope, built a stone temple of Ares what time they went forth to war. Now here an unspeakable help will come to you from the bitter sea; wherefore with kindly intent I bid you stay. But what need is there that I should sin yet again declaring everything to the end by my prophetic art? And beyond the island and opposite mainland dwell the Philyres: and above the Philyres are the Macrones, and after them the vast tribes of the Becheiri. And next in order to them dwell the Sapeires, and the Byzeres have the lands adjoining to them, and beyond them at last live the warlike Colchians themselves. But speed on in your ship, till ye touch the inmost bourne of the sea. And here at the Cytaean mainland and from the Amarantine mountains far away and the Circaean plain eddying Phasis rolls his broad stream to the sea. Guide your ship to the mouth of that river and ye shall behold the towers of Cytaean Aeetes and the shady grove of Ares, where a dragon, a monster terrible to behold, ever glares around, keeping watch over the fleece that is spread upon the top of an oak; neither by day nor by night does sweet sleep subdue his restless eyes."

Thus he spake, and straightway fear seized them as they heard. And for a long while they were struck with silence; till at last the hero, son of Aeson, spake, sore dismayed at their evil plight:

"O aged sire, now hast thou come to the end of the toils of our sea-journeying and hast told us the token, trusting to which we shall make our way to Pontus through the hateful rocks; but whether, when we have escaped them, we shall have a return back again to Hellas, this too would we gladly learn from thee. What shall I do, how shall I go over again such a long path through the sea, unskilled as I am, with unskilled comrades? And Colchian Aea lies at the edge of Pontus and of the world."

Thus he spake, and him the aged sire addressed in reply: "O son, when once thou hast escaped through the deadly rocks, fear not; for a deity will be the guide from Aea by another track; and to Aea there will be guides enough. But, my friends, take thought of the artful aid of the Cyprian goddess. For on her depends the glorious issue of your venture. And further than this ask me not."

Thus spake Agenor's son, and close at hand the twin sons of Thracian Boreas came darting from the sky and set their swift feet upon the threshold; and the heroes rose up from their seats when they saw them present. And Zetes, still drawing hard breath after his toil, spake among the eager listeners, telling them how far they had driven the Harpies and how Iris prevented their slaying them, and how the goddess of her grace gave them pledges, and how those others in fear plunged into the vast cave of the Dictaean cliff. Then in the mansion all their comrades were joyful at the tidings and so was Phineus himself. And quickly Aeson's son, with good will exceeding, addressed him:

"Assuredly there was then, Phineus, some god who cared for thy bitter woe, and brought us hither from afar, that the sons of Boreas might aid thee; and if too he should bring sight to thine eyes, verily I should rejoice, methinks, as much as if I were on my homeward way."

Thus he spake, but Phineus replied to him with downcast look: "Son of Aeson, that is past recall, nor is there any remedy hereafter, for blasted are my sightless eyes. But instead of that, may the god grant me death at once, and after death I shall take my share in perfect bliss."

Then they two returned answering speech, each to other, and soon in the midst of their converse early dawn appeared; and round Phineus were gathered the neighbours who used to come thither aforetime day by day and constantly bring a portion of their food. To all alike, however poor he was that came, the aged man gave his oracles with good will, and freed many from their woes by his prophetic art; wherefore they visited and tended him. And with them came Paraebius, who was dearest to him, and gladly did he perceive these strangers in the house. For long ere now the seer himself had said that a band of chieftains, faring from Hellas to the city of Aeetes, would make fast their hawsers to the Thynian land, and by Zeus' will would check the approach of the Harpies. The rest the old man pleased with words of wisdom and let them go; Paraebius only he bade remain there with the chiefs; and straightway he sent him and bade him bring back the choicest of his sheep. And when he had left the hall Phineus spake gently amid the throng of oarsmen:

"O my friends, not all men are arrogant, it seems, nor unmindful of benefits. Even as this man, loyal as he is, came hither to learn his fate. For when he laboured the most and toiled the most, then the needs of life, ever growing more and more, would waste him, and day after day ever dawned more wretched, nor was there any respite to his toil. But he was paying the sad penalty of his father's sin. For he when alone on the mountains, felling trees, once slighted the prayers of a Hamadryad, who wept and sought to soften him with plaintive words, not to cut down the stump of an oak tree coeval with herself, wherein for a long time she had lived continually; but he in the arrogance of youth recklessly cut it down. So to him the nymph thereafter made her death a curse, to him and to his children. I indeed knew of the sin when he came; and I bid him build an altar to the Thynian nymph, and offer on it an atoning sacrifice, with prayer to escape his father's fate. Here, ever since he escaped the god-sent doom, never has he forgotten or neglected me; but sorely and against his will do I send him from my doors, so eager is he to remain with me in my affliction."

Thus spake Agenor's son; and his friend straightway came near leading two sheep from the flock. And up rose Jason and up rose the sons of Boreas at the bidding of the aged sire. And quickly they called upon Apollo, lord of prophecy, and offered sacrifice upon the hearth as the day was just sinking. And the younger comrades made ready a feast to their hearts' desire. Thereupon having well feasted they turned themselves to rest, some near the ship's hawsers, others in groups throughout the mansion. And at dawn the Etesian winds blew strongly, which by the command of Zeus blow over every land equally.

Cyrene, the tale goes, once tended sheep along the marsh-meadow of Peneus among men of old time; for dear to her were maidenhood and a couch unstained. But, as she guarded her flock by the river, Apollo carried her off far from Haemonia and placed her among the nymphs of the land, who dwelt in Libya near the Myrtosian height. And here to Phoebus she bore Aristaeus whom the Haemonians, rich in corn-land, call "Hunter" and "Shepherd." Her, of his love, the god made a nymph there, of long life and a huntress, and his son he brought while still an infant to be nurtured in the cave of Cheiron. And to him when he grew to manhood the Muses gave a bride, and taught him the arts of healing and of prophecy; and they made him the keeper of their sheep, of all that grazed on the Athamantian plain of Phthia and round steep Othrys and the sacred stream of the river Apidanus. But when from heaven Sirius scorched the Minoan Isles, and for long there was no respite for the inhabitants, then by the injunction of the Far-Darter they summoned Aristaeus to ward off the pestilence. And by his father's command he left Phthia and made his home in Ceos, and gathered together the Parrhasian people who are of the lineage of Lycaon, and he built a great altar to Zeus Icmaeus, and duly offered sacrifices upon the mountains to that star Sirius, and to Zeus son of Cronos himself. And on this account it is that Etesian winds from Zeus cool the land for forty days, and in Ceos even now the priests offer sacrifices before the rising of the Dog-star.

So the tale is told, but the chieftains stayed there by constraint, and every day the Thynians, doing pleasure to Phineus, sent them gifts beyond measure. And afterwards they raised an altar to the blessed twelve on the sea-beach opposite and laid offerings thereon and then entered their swift ship to row, nor did they forget to bear with them a trembling dove; but Euphemus seized her and brought her all quivering with fear, and they loosed the twin hawsers from the land.

Nor did they start unmarked by Athena, but straightway swiftly she set her feet on a light cloud, which would waft her on, mighty though she was, and she swept on to the sea with friendly thoughts to the oarsmen. And as when one roveth far from his native land, as we men often wander with enduring heart, nor is any land too distant but all ways are clear to his view, and he sees in mind his own home, and at once the way over sea and land seems plain, and swiftly thinking, now this way, now that, he strains with eager eyes; so swiftly the daughter of Zeus darted down and set her foot on the cheerless shore of Thynia.

Now when they reached the narrow strait of the winding passage, hemmed in on both sides by rugged cliffs, while an eddying current from below was washing against the ship as she moved on, they went forward sorely in dread; and now the thud of the crashing rocks ceaselessly struck their ears, and the sea-washed shores resounded, and then Euphemus grasped the dove in his hand and started to mount the prow; and they, at the bidding of Tiphys, son of Hagnias, rowed with good will to drive *Argo* between the rocks, trusting to their strength. And as they rounded a bend they saw the rocks opening for the last time of all. Their spirit melted within them; and Euphemus sent forth the dove to dart forward in flight; and they all together raised their heads to look; but she flew between them, and the rocks again rushed together and crashed as they met face to face. And the foam leapt up in a mass like a cloud; awful was the thunder of the sea; and all round them the mighty welkin roared.

The hollow caves beneath the rugged cliffs rumbled as the sea came surging in; and the white foam of the dashing wave spurted high above the cliff. Next the current whirled the ship round. And the rocks shore away the end of the dove's tail-feathers; but away she flew unscathed. And the rowers gave a loud cry; and Tiphys himself called to them to row with might and main. For the rocks were again parting asunder. But as they rowed they trembled, until the tide returning drove them back within the rocks. Then most awful fear seized upon all; for over their head was destruction without escape. And now to right and left broad Pontus was seen, when suddenly a huge wave rose up before them, arched, like a steep rock; and at the sight they bowed with bended heads. For it seemed about to leap down upon the ship's whole length and to overwhelm them. But Tiphys was quick to ease the ship as she laboured with the oars; and in all its mass the wave rolled away beneath the keel, and at the stern it raised *Argo* herself and drew her far away from the rocks; and high in air was she borne. But Euphemus strode among all his comrades and cried to them to bend to their oars with all their might; and they with a shout smote the water. And as far as the ship yielded to the rowers, twice as far did she leap back, and the oars were bent like curved bows as the heroes used their strength.

Then a vaulted billow rushed upon them, and the ship like a cylinder ran on the furious wave plunging through the hollow sea. And the eddying current held her between the clashing rocks; and on each side they shook and thundered; and the ship's timbers were held fast. Then Athena with her left hand thrust back one mighty rock and with her right pushed the ship through; and she, like a winged arrow, sped through the air. Nevertheless the rocks, ceaselessly clashing, shore off as she passed the extreme end of the stern-ornament. But Athena soared up to Olympus, when they had escaped unscathed. And the rocks in one spot at that moment were rooted fast for ever to each other, which thing had been destined by the blessed gods, when a man in his ship should have passed between them alive. And the heroes breathed again after their chilling fear, beholding at the same time the sky and the expanse of sea spreading far and wide. For they deemed that they were saved from Hades; and Tiphys first of all began to speak:

"It is my hope that we have safely escaped this peril—we, and the ship; and none other is the cause so much as Athena, who breathed into

Argo divine strength when Argus knitted her together with bolts; and she may not be caught. Son of Aeson, no longer fear thou so much the best of thy king, since a god hath granted us escape between the rocks; for Phineus, Agenor's son, said that our toils hereafter would be lightly accomplished."

He spake, and at once he sped the ship onward through the midst of the sea past the Bithynian coast. But Jason with gentle words addressed him in reply: "Tiphys, why dost thou comfort thus my grieving heart? I have erred and am distraught in wretched and helpless ruin. For I ought, when Pelias gave the command, to have straightway refused this quest to his face, yea, though I were doomed to die pitilessly, torn limb from limb, but now I am wrapped in excessive fear and cares unbearable, dreading to sail through the chilling paths of the sea, and dreading when we shall set foot on the mainland. For on every side are unkindly men. And ever when day is done I pass a night of groans from the time when ye first gathered together for my sake, while I take thought for all things; but thou talkest at thine ease, caring only for thine own life; while for myself I am dismayed not a whit; but I fear for this man and for that equally, and for thee, and for my other comrades, if I shall not bring you back safe to the land of Hellas."

Thus he spake, making trial of the chiefs; but they shouted loud with cheerful words. And his heart was warmed within him at their cry and again he spake outright among them: "My friends, in your valour my courage is quickened. Wherefore now, even though I should take my way through the gulfs of Hades, no more shall I let fear seize upon me, since ye are steadfast amid cruel terrors. But now that we have sailed out from the striking rocks, I trow that never hereafter will there be another such fearful thing, if indeed we go on our way following the counsel of Phineus."

Thus he spake, and straightway they ceased from such words and gave unwearying labour to the oar; and quickly they passed by the swiftly flowing river Rhebas and the peak of Colone, and soon thereafter the black headland, and near it the mouth of the river Phyllis, where aforetime Dipsacus received in his home the son of Athamas, when with his ram he was flying from the city of Orchomenus; and Dipsacus was the son of a meadow-nymph, nor was insolence his delight, but contented by his father's stream he dwelt with his mother, pasturing his flocks by the shore. And quickly they sighted and sailed past his shrine and the broad banks of the river and the plain, and deep-flowing Calpe, and all the windless night and the day they bent to their tireless oars. And even as ploughing oxen toil as they cleave the moist earth, and sweat streams in abundance from flank and neck; and from beneath the yoke their eyes roll askance, while the breath ever rushes from their mouths in hot gasps; and all day long they toil, planting their hoofs deep in the ground; like them the heroes kept dragging their oars through the sea.

Now when divine light has not yet come nor is it utter darkness, but a faint glimmer has spread over the night, the time when men wake and call it twilight, at that hour they ran into the harbour of the desert island Thynias and, spent by weary toil, mounted the shore. And to them the son of Leto, as he passed from Lycia far away to the countless folk of the Hyperboreans, appeared; and about his cheeks on both sides his golden locks flowed in clusters as he moved; in his left hand he held a silver bow, and on his back was slung a quiver hanging from his shoulders; and beneath his feet all the island quaked, and the waves surged high on the beach. Helpless amazement seized them as they looked; and no one dared to gaze face to face into the fair eyes of the god. And they stood with heads bowed to the ground; but he, far off, passed on to the sea through the air; and at length Orpheus spake as follows, addressing the chiefs:

"Come, let us call this island the sacred isle of Apollo of the Dawn since he has appeared to all, passing by at dawn; and we will offer such sacrifices as we can, building an altar on the shore; and if hereafter he shall grant us a safe return to the Haemonian land, then will we lay on his altar the thighs of horned goats. And now I bid you propitiate him with the steam of sacrifice and libations. Be gracious, O king, be gracious in thy appearing."

Thus he spake, and they straightway built up an altar with shingle; and over the island they wandered, seeking if haply they could get a glimpse of a fawn or a wild goat, that often seek their pasture in the deep wood. And for them Leto's son provided a quarry; and with pious rites they wrapped in fat the thigh bones of them all and burnt them on the sacred altar, celebrating Apollo, Lord of Dawn. And round the burning sacrifice they set up a broad dancing-ring, singing, "All hail, fair god of healing, Phoebus, all hail," and with them Oeagrus' goodly son began a clear lay on his Bistonian lyre; how once beneath the rocky ridge of Parnassus he slew with his bow the monster Delphyne, he, still young and beardless, still rejoicing in his long tresses. Mayst thou be gracious! Ever, O king, be thy locks unshorn, ever unravaged; for so is it right. And none but Leto, daughter of Coeus, strokes them with her dear hands. And often the Corycian nymphs, daughters of Pleistus, took up the cheering strain crying "Healer"; hence arose this lovely refrain of the hymn to Phoebus.

Now when they had celebrated him with dance and song they took an oath with holy libations, that they would ever help each other with concord of heart, touching the sacrifice as they swore; and even now there stands there a temple to gracious Concord, which the heroes themselves reared, paying honour at that time to the glorious goddess.

Now when the third morning came, with a fresh west wind they left the lofty island. Next, on the opposite side they saw and passed the mouth of the river Sangarius and the fertile land of the Mariandyni, and the stream of Lycus and the Anthemoeisian lake; and beneath the breeze the ropes and all the tackling quivered as they sped onward. During the night the wind ceased and at dawn they gladly reached the haven of the Acherusian headland. It rises aloft with steep cliffs, looking towards the Bithynian sea; and beneath it smooth rocks, ever washed by the sea, stand rooted firm; and round them the wave rolls and thunders loud, but above, wide-spreading plane trees grow on the topmost point. And from it towards the land a hollow glen slopes gradually away, where there is a cave of Hades overarched by wood and rocks. From here an icy breath, unceasingly issuing from the chill recess, ever forms a glistening rime which melts again beneath the midday sun. And never does silence hold that grim headland, but there is a continual murmur from the sounding sea and the leaves that quiver in the winds from the cave. And here is the outfall of the river Acheron which bursts its way through the headland and falls into the Eastern sea, and a hollow ravine brings it down from above. In after times the Nisaean Megarians named it Soönautes[15] when they were about to settle in the land of the Mariandyni. For indeed the river saved them with their ships when they were caught in a violent tempest. By this way the heroes took the ship through[16] the Acherusian headland and came to land over against it as the wind had just ceased.

Not long had they come unmarked by Lycus, the lord of that land, and the Mariandyni—they, the slayers of Amycus, according to the

---

15. i.e. Saviour of sailors.
16. i.e. through the ravine that divides the headland.

report which the people heard before; but for that very deed they even made a league with the heroes. And Polydeuces himself they welcomed as a god, flocking from every side, since for a long time had they been warring against the arrogant Bebrycians. And so they went up all together into the city, and all that day with friendly feelings made ready a feast within the palace of Lycus and gladdened their souls with converse. Aeson's son told him the lineage and name of each of his comrades and the behests of Pelias, and how they were welcomed by the Lemnian women, and all that they did at Dolionian Cyzicus; and how they reached the Mysian land and Cius, where, sore against their will, they left behind the hero Heracles, and he told the saying of Glaucus, and how they slew the Bebrycians and Amycus, and he told of the prophecies and affliction of Phineus, and how they escaped the Cyanean rocks, and how they met with Leto's son at the island. And as he told all, Lycus was charmed in soul with listening; and he grieved for Heracles left behind, and spake as follows among them all:

"O friends, what a man he was from whose help ye have fallen away, as ye cleave your long path to Aeetes; for well do I know that I saw him here in the halls of Dascylus my father, when he came hither on foot through the land of Asia bringing the girdle of warlike Hippolyte; and me he found with the down just growing on my cheeks. And here, when my brother Priolas was slain by the Mysians—my brother, whom ever since the people lament with most piteous dirges—he entered the lists with Titias in boxing and slew him, mighty Titias, who surpassed all the youths in beauty and strength; and he dashed his teeth to the ground. Together with the Mysians he subdued beneath my father's sway the Phrygians also, who inhabit the lands next to us, and he made his own the tribes of the Bithynians and their land, as far as the mouth of Rhebas and the peak of Colone; and besides them the Paphlagonians of Pelops yielded just as they were, even all those round whom the dark water of Billaeus breaks. But now the Bebrycians and the insolence of Amycus have robbed me, since Heracles dwells far away, for they have long been cutting off huge pieces of my land until they have set their bounds at the meadows of deep-flowing Hypius. Nevertheless, by your hands have they paid the penalty; and it was not without the will of heaven, I trow, that he brought war on the Bebrycians this day—he, the son of Tyndareus, when he slew that champion. Wherefore whatever requital I am now able to pay, gladly will I pay it, for that is the rule for weaker men when the stronger begin to help them. So with you all, and in your company, I bid Dascylus my son follow; and if he goes, you will find all men friendly that ye meet on your way through the sea even to the mouth of the river Thermodon. And besides that, to the sons of Tyndareus will I raise a lofty temple on the Acherusian height, which all sailors shall mark far across the sea and shall reverence; and hereafter for them will I set apart outside the city, as for gods, some fertile fields of the well-tilled plain."

Thus all day long they revelled at the banquet. But at dawn they hied down to the ship in haste; and with them went Lycus himself, when he had given them countless gifts to bear away; and with them he sent forth his son from his home.

And here his destined fate smote Idmon, son of Abas, skilled in soothsaying; but not at all did his soothsaying save him, for necessity drew him on to death. For in the mead of the reedy river there lay, cooling his flanks and huge belly in the mud, a white-tusked boar, a deadly monster, whom even the nymphs of the marsh dreaded, and no man knew it; but all alone he was feeding in the wide fen. But the son of Abas was passing along the raised banks of the muddy river, and the boar from some unseen lair leapt out of the reed-bed, and charging gashed his thigh and severed in twain the sinews and the bone. And with a sharp cry the hero fell to the ground; and as he was struck his comrades flocked together with answering cry. And quickly Peleus with his hunting spear aimed at the murderous boar as he fled back into the fen; and again he turned and charged; but Idas wounded him, and with a roar he fell impaled upon the sharp spear. And the boar they left on the ground just as he had fallen there; but Idmon, now at the last gasp, his comrades bore to the ship in sorrow of heart, and he died in his comrades' arms.

And here they stayed from taking thought for their voyaging and abode in grief for the burial of their dead friend. And for three whole days they lamented; and on the next they buried him with full honours, and the people and King Lycus himself took part in the funeral rites; and, as is the due of the departed, they slaughtered countless sheep at his tomb. And so a barrow to this hero was raised in that land, and there stands a token for men of later days to see, the trunk of a wild olive tree, such as ships are built of; and it flourishes with its green leaves a little below the Acherusian headland. And if at the bidding of the Muses I must tell this tale outright, Phoebus strictly commanded the Boeotians and Nisaeans to worship him as guardian of their city, and to build their city round the trunk of the ancient wild olive; but they, instead of the god-fearing Aeolid Idmon, at this day honour Agamestor.

Who was the next that died? For then a second time the heroes heaped up a barrow for a comrade dead. For still are to be seen two monuments of those heroes. The tale goes that Tiphys son of Hagnias died; nor was it his destiny thereafter to sail any further. But him there on the spot a short sickness laid to rest far from his native land, when the company had paid due honours to the dead son of Abas. And at the cruel woe they were seized with unbearable grief. For when with due honours they had buried him also hard by the seer, they cast themselves down in helplessness on the sea-shore silently, closely wrapped up, and took no thought for meat or drink; and their spirit drooped in grief, for all hope of return was gone. And in their sorrow they would have stayed from going further had not Hera kindled exceeding courage in Ancaeus, whom near the waters of Imbrasus Astypalaea bore to Poseidon; for especially was he skilled in steering and eagerly did he address Peleus:

"Son of Aeacus, is it well for us to give up our toils and linger on in a strange land? Not so much for my prowess in war did Jason take me with him in quest of the fleece, far from Parthenia, as for my knowledge of ships. Wherefore, I pray, let there be no fear for the ship. And so there are here other men of skill, of whom none will harm our voyaging, whomsoever we set at the helm. But quickly tell forth all this and boldly urge them to call to mind their task."

Thus he spake; and Peleus' soul was stirred with gladness, and straightway he spake in the midst of all: "My friends, why do we thus cherish a bootless grief like this? For those two have perished by the fate they have met with; but among our host are steersmen yet, and many a one. Wherefore let us not delay our attempt, but rouse yourselves to the work and cast away your griefs."

And him in reply Aeson's son addressed with helpless words: "Son of Aeacus, where are these steersmen of thine? For those whom we once deemed to be men of skill, they even more than I are bowed with vexation of heart. Wherefore I forebode an evil doom for us even as for the dead, if it shall be our lot neither to reach the city of fell Aeetes, nor ever again to pass beyond the rocks to the land of Hellas, but a wretched fate will enshroud us here ingloriously till we grow old for naught."

Thus he spake, but Ancaeus quickly undertook to guide the swift ship; for he was stirred by the impulse of the goddess. And after him

Erginus and Nauplius and Euphemus started up, eager to steer. But the others held them back, and many of his comrades granted it to Ancaeus.

So on the twelfth day they went aboard at dawn, for a strong breeze of westerly wind was blowing. And quickly with the oars they passed out through the river Acheron and, trusting to the wind, shook out their sails, and with canvas spread far and wide they were cleaving their passage through the waves in fair weather. And soon they passed the outfall of the river Callichorus, where, as the tale goes, the Nysean son of Zeus, when he had left the tribes of the Indians and came to dwell at Thebes, held revels and arrayed dances in front of a cave, wherein he passed unsmiling sacred nights, from which time the neighbours call the river by the name of Callichorus[17] and the cave Aulion.[18]

Next they beheld the barrow of Sthenelus, Actor's son, who on his way back from the valorous war against the Amazons—for he had been the comrade of Heracles—was struck by an arrow and died there upon the sea-beach. And for a time they went no further, for Persephone herself sent forth the spirit of Actor's son which craved with many tears to behold men like himself, even for a moment. And mounting on the edge of the barrow he gazed upon the ship, such as he was when he went to war; and round his head a fair helm with four peaks gleamed with its blood-red crest. And again he entered the vast gloom; and they looked and marvelled; and Mopsus, son of Ampycus, with word of prophecy urged them to land and propitiate him with libations. Quickly they drew in sail and threw out hawsers, and on the strand paid honour to the tomb of Sthenelus, and poured out drink offerings to him and sacrificed sheep as victims. And besides the drink offerings they built an altar to Apollo, saviour of ships, and burnt thigh bones; and Orpheus dedicated his lyre; whence the place has the name of Lyra.

And straightway they went aboard as the wind blew strong; and they drew the sail down, and made it taut to both sheets; then *Argo* was borne over the sea swiftly, even as a hawk soaring high through the air commits to the breeze its outspread wings and is borne on swiftly, nor swerves in its flight, poising in the clear sky with quiet pinions. And lo, they passed by the stream of Parthenius as it flows into the sea, a most gentle river, where the maid, daughter of Leto, when she mounts to heaven after the chase, cools her limbs in its much-desired waters. Then

17. i.e. river of fair dances.
18. i.e. the bedchamber.

APOLLONIUS OF RHODES

they sped onward in the night without ceasing, and passed Sesamus and lofty Erythini, Crobialus, Cromna and woody Cytorus. Next they swept round Carambis at the rising of the sun, and plied the oars past long Aegialus, all day and on through the night.

And straightway they landed on the Assyrian shore where Zeus himself gave a home to Sinope, daughter of Asopus, and granted her virginity, beguiled by his own promises. For he longed for her love, and he promised to grant her whatever her heart's desire might be. And she in her craftiness asked of him virginity. And in like manner she deceived Apollo too who longed to wed her, and besides them the river Halys, and no man ever subdued her in love's embrace. And there the sons of noble Deimachus of Tricca were still dwelling, Deileon, Autolycus and Phlogius, since the day when they wandered far away from Heracles; and they, when they marked the array of chieftains, went to meet them and declared in truth who they were; and they wished to remain there no longer, but as soon as Argestes[19] blew went on ship-board. And so with them, borne along by the swift breeze, the heroes left behind the river Halys, and left behind Iris that flows hard by, and the delta-land of Assyria; and on the same day they rounded the distant headland of the Amazons that guards their harbour.

Here once when Melanippe, daughter of Ares, had gone forth, the hero Heracles caught her by ambuscade and Hippolyte gave him her glistening girdle as her sister's ransom, and he sent away his captive unharmed. In the bay of this headland, at the outfall of Thermodon, they ran ashore, for the sea was rough for their voyage. No river is like this, and none sends forth from itself such mighty streams over the land. If a man should count every one he would lack but four of a hundred, but the real spring is only one. This flows down to the plain from lofty mountains, which, men say, are called the Amazonian mountains. Thence it spreads inland over a hilly country straight forward; wherefrom its streams go winding on, and they roll on, this way and that ever more, wherever best they can reach the lower ground, one at a distance and another near at hand; and many streams are swallowed up in the sand and are without a name; but, mingled with a few, the main stream openly bursts with its arching crest of foam into the Inhospitable Pontus. And they would have tarried there and have closed in battle with the Amazons, and would have fought not without

---

19. The north-west wind.

bloodshed—for the Amazons were not gentle foes and regarded not justice, those dwellers on the Doeantian plain; but grievous insolence and the works of Ares were all their care; for by race they were the daughters of Ares and the nymph Harmonia, who bare to Ares war-loving maids, wedded to him in the glens of the Acmonian wood—had not the breezes of Argestes come again from Zeus; and with the wind they left the rounded beach, where the Themiscyreian Amazons were arming for war. For they dwelt not gathered together in one city, but scattered over the land, parted into three tribes. In one part dwelt the Themiscyreians, over whom at that time Hippolyte reigned, in another the Lycastians, and in another the dart-throwing Chadesians. And the next day they sped on and at nightfall they reached the land of the Chalybes.

That folk have no care for ploughing with oxen or for any planting of honey-sweet fruit; nor yet do they pasture flocks in the dewy meadow. But they cleave the hard iron-bearing land and exchange their wages for daily sustenance; never does the morn rise for them without toil, but amid bleak sooty flames and smoke they endure heavy labour.

And straightway thereafter they rounded the headland of Genetaean Zeus and sped safely past the land of the Tibareni. Here when wives bring forth children to their husbands, the men lie in bed and groan with their heads close bound; but the women tend them with food, and prepare child-birth baths for them.

Next they reached the sacred mount and the land where the Mossynoeci dwell amid high mountains in wooden huts,[20] from which that people take their name. And strange are their customs and laws. Whatever it is right to do openly before the people or in the market place, all this they do in their homes, but whatever acts we perform at home, these they perform out of doors in the midst of the streets, without blame. And among them is no reverence for the marriage-bed, but, like swine that feed in herds, no whit abashed in others' presence, on the earth they lie with the women. Their king sits in the loftiest hut and dispenses upright judgments to the multitude, poor wretch! For if haply he err at all in his decrees, for that day they keep him shut up in starvation.

They passed them by and cleft their way with oars over against the island of Ares all day long; for at dusk the light breeze left them. At last they spied above them, hurtling through the air, one of the birds

---

20. called "Mossynes."

of Ares which haunt that isle. It shook its wings down over the ship as she sped on and sent against her a keen feather, and it fell on the left shoulder of goodly Oileus, and he dropped his oar from his hands at the sudden blow, and his comrades marvelled at the sight of the winged bolt. And Eribotes from his seat hard by drew out the feather, and bound up the wound when he had loosed the strap hanging from his own sword-sheath; and besides the first, another bird appeared swooping down; but the hero Clytius, son of Eurytus—for he bent his curved bow, and sped a swift arrow against the bird—struck it, and it whirled round and fell close to the ship. And to them spake Amphidamas, son of Aleus:

"The island of Ares is near us; you know it yourselves now that ye have seen these birds. But little will arrows avail us, I trow, for landing. But let us contrive some other device to help us, if ye intend to land, bearing in mind the injunction of Phineus. For not even could Heracles, when he came to Arcadia, drive away with bow and arrow the birds that swam on the Stymphalian lake. I saw it myself. But he shook in his hand a rattle of bronze and made a loud clatter as he stood upon a lofty peak; and the birds fled far off, screeching in bewildered fear. Wherefore now too let us contrive some such device, and I myself will speak, having pondered the matter beforehand. Set on your heads your helmets of lofty crest, then half row by turns, and half fence the ship about with polished spears and shields. Then all together raise a mighty shout so that the birds may be scared by the unwonted din, the nodding crests, and the uplifted spears on high. And if we reach the island itself, then make mighty noise with the clashing of shields."

Thus he spake, and the helpful device pleased all. And on their heads they placed helmets of bronze, gleaming terribly, and the blood-red crests were tossing. And half of them rowed in turn, and the rest covered the ship with spears and shields. And as when a man roofs over a house with tiles, to be an ornament of his home and a defence against rain, and one tile fits firmly into another, each after each; so they roofed over the ship with their shields, locking them together. And as a din arises from a warrior-host of men sweeping on, when lines of battle meet, such a shout rose upward from the ship into the air. Now they saw none of the birds yet, but when they touched the island and clashed upon their shields, then the birds in countless numbers rose in flight hither and thither. And as when the son of Cronos sends from the clouds a dense hail storm on city and houses, and the people who dwell beneath hear the din above the roof and sit quietly, since the stormy season has not come upon them unawares, but they have first made strong their roofs; so the birds sent against the heroes a thick shower of feather-shafts as they darted over the sea to the mountains of the land opposite.

What then was the purpose of Phineus in bidding the divine band of heroes land there? Or what kind of help was about to meet their desire?

The sons of Phrixus were faring towards the city of Orchomenus from Aea, coming from Cytaean Aeetes, on board a Colchian ship, to win the boundless wealth of their father; for he, when dying, had enjoined this journey upon them. And lo, on that day they were very near that island. But Zeus had impelled the north wind's might to blow, marking by rain the moist path of Arcturus; and all day long he was stirring the leaves upon the mountains, breathing gently upon the topmost sprays; but at night he rushed upon the sea with monstrous force, and with his shrieking blasts uplifted the surge; and a dark mist covered the heavens, nor did the bright stars anywhere appear from among the clouds, but a murky gloom brooded all around. And so the sons of Phrixus, drenched and trembling in fear of a horrible doom, were borne along by the waves helplessly. And the force of the wind had snatched away their sails and shattered in twain the hull, tossed as it was by the breakers. And hereupon by heaven's prompting those four clutched a huge beam, one of many that were scattered about, held together by sharp bolts, when the ship broke to pieces. And on to the island the waves and the blasts of wind bore the men in their distress, within a little of death. And straightway a mighty rain burst forth, and rained upon the sea and the island, and all the country opposite the island, where the arrogant Mossynoeci dwelt. And the sweep of the waves hurled the sons of Phrixus, together with their massy beam, upon the beach of the island, in the murky night; and the floods of rain from Zeus ceased at sunrise, and soon the two bands drew near and met each other, and Argus spoke first:

"We beseech you, by Zeus the Beholder, whoever ye are, to be kindly and to help us in our need. For fierce tempests, falling on the sea, have shattered all the timbers of the crazy ship in which we were cleaving our path on business bent. Wherefore we entreat you, if haply ye will listen, to grant us just a covering for our bodies, and to pity and succour men in misfortune, your equals in age. Oh, reverence suppliants and strangers for Zeus' sake, the god of strangers and suppliants. To Zeus belong both suppliants and strangers; and his eye, methinks, beholdeth even us."

And in reply the son of Aeson prudently questioned him, deeming that the prophecies of Phineus were being fulfilled: "All these things will we straightway grant you with right good will. But come tell me truly in what country ye dwell and what business bids you sail across the sea, and tell me your own glorious names and lineage."

And him Argus, helpless in his evil plight, addressed: "That one Phrixus an Aeolid reached Aea from Hellas you yourselves have clearly heard ere this, I trow; Phrixus, who came to the city of Aeetes, bestriding a ram, which Hermes had made all gold; and the fleece ye may see even now. The ram, at its own prompting, he then sacrificed to Zeus, son of Cronos, above all, the god of fugitives. And him did Aeetes receive in his palace, and with gladness of heart gave him his daughter Chalciope in marriage without gifts of wooing.[21] From those two are we sprung. But Phrixus died at last, an aged man, in the home of Aeetes; and we, giving heed to our father's behests, are journeying to Orchomenus to take the possessions of Athamas. And if thou dost desire to learn our names, this is Cytissorus, this Phrontis, and this Melas, and me ye may call Argus."

Thus he spake, and the chieftains rejoiced at the meeting, and tended them, much marvelling. And Jason again in turn replied, as was fitting, with these words:

"Surely ye are our kinsmen on my father's side, and ye pray that with kindly hearts we succour your evil plight. For Cretheus and Athamas were brothers. I am the grandson of Cretheus, and with these comrades here I am journeying from that same Hellas to the city of Aeetes. But of these things we will converse hereafter. And do ye first put clothing upon you. By heaven's devising, I ween, have ye come to my hands in your sore need."

He spake, and out of the ship gave them raiment to put on. Then all together they went to the temple of Ares to offer sacrifice of sheep; and in haste they stood round the altar, which was outside the roofless temple, an altar built of pebbles; within a black stone stood fixed, a sacred thing, to which of yore the Amazons all used to pray. Nor was it lawful for them, when they came from the opposite coast, to burn on

---

21. i.e. without exacting gifts from the bridegroom. So in the Iliad (ix. 146) Agamemnon offers Achilles any of his three daughters

this altar offerings of sheep and oxen, but they used to slay horses which they kept in great herds. Now when they had sacrificed and eaten the feast prepared, then Aeson's son spake among them and thus began:

"Zeus' self, I ween, beholds everything; nor do we men escape his eye, we that be god-fearing and just, for as he rescued your father from the hands of a murderous step-dame and gave him measureless wealth besides; even so hath he saved you harmless from the baleful storm. And on board this ship ye may sail hither and thither, where ye will, whether to Aea or to the wealthy city of divine Orchomenus. For our ship Athena built and with axe of bronze cut her timbers near the crest of Pelion, and with the goddess wrought Argus. But yours the fierce surge hath shattered, before ye came nigh to the rocks which all day long clash together in the straits of the sea. But come, be yourselves our helpers, for we are eager to bring to Hellas the golden fleece, and guide us on our voyage, for I go to atone for the intended sacrifice of Phrixus, the cause of Zeus' wrath against the sons of Aeolus."

He spake with soothing words; but horror seized them when they heard. For they deemed that they would not find Aeetes friendly if they desired to take away the ram's fleece. And Argus spake as follows, vexed that they should busy themselves with such a quest:

"My friends, our strength, so far as it avails, shall never cease to help you, not one whit, when need shall come. But Aeetes is terribly armed with deadly ruthlessness; wherefore exceedingly do I dread this voyage. And he boasts himself to be the son of Helios; and all round dwell countless tribes of Colchians; and he might match himself with Ares in his dread war-cry and giant strength. Nay, to seize the fleece in spite of Aeetes is no easy task; so huge a serpent keeps guard round and about it, deathless and sleepless, which Earth herself brought forth on the sides of Caucasus, by the rock of Typhaon, where Typhaon, they say, smitten by the bolt of Zeus, son of Cronos, when he lifted against the god his sturdy hands, dropped from his head hot gore; and in such plight he reached the mountains and plain of Nysa, where to this day he lies whelmed beneath the waters of the Serbonian lake."

Thus he spake, and straightway many a cheek grew pale when they heard of so mighty an adventure. But quickly Peleus answered with cheering words, and thus spake:

"Be not so fearful in spirit, my good friend. For we are not so lacking in prowess as to be no match for Aeetes to try his strength with arms; but I deem that we too are cunning in war, we that go thither, near akin to the blood of the blessed gods. Wherefore if he will not grant us the fleece of gold for friendship's sake, the tribes of the Colchians will not avail him, I ween."

Thus they addressed each other in turn, until again, satisfied with their feast, they turned to rest. And when they rose at dawn a gentle breeze was blowing; and they raised the sails, which strained to the rush of the wind, and quickly they left behind the island of Ares.

And at nightfall they came to the island of Philyra, where Cronos, son of Uranus, what time in Olympus he reigned over the Titans, and Zeus was yet being nurtured in a Cretan cave by the Curetes of Ida, lay beside Philyra, when he had deceived Rhea; and the goddess found them in the midst of their dalliance; and Cronos leapt up from the couch with a rush in the form of a steed with flowing mane, but Ocean's daughter, Philyra, in shame left the spot and those haunts, and came to the long Pelasgian ridges, where by her union with the transfigured deity she brought forth huge Cheiron, half like a horse, half like a god.

Thence they sailed on, past the Macrones and the far-stretching land of the Becheiri and the overweening Sapeires, and after them the Byzeres; for ever forward they clave their way, quickly borne by the gentle breeze. And lo, as they sped on, a deep gulf of the sea was opened, and lo, the steep crags of the Caucasian mountains rose up, where, with his limbs bound upon the hard rocks by galling fetters of bronze, Prometheus fed with his liver an eagle that ever rushed back to its prey. High above the ship at even they saw it flying with a loud whirr, near the clouds; and yet it shook all the sails with the fanning of those huge wings. For it had not the form of a bird of the air but kept poising its long wing-feathers like polished oars. And not long after they heard the bitter cry of Prometheus as his liver was being torn away; and the air rang with his screams until they marked the ravening eagle rushing back from the mountain on the self-same track. And at night, by the skill of Argus, they reached broad-flowing Phasis, and the utmost bourne of the sea.

And straightway they let down the sails and the yard-arm and stowed them inside the hollow mast-crutch, and at once they lowered the mast itself till it lay along; and quickly with oars they entered the mighty stream of the river; and round the prow the water surged as it gave them way. And on their left hand they had lofty Caucasus and the Cytaean city of Aea, and on the other side the plain of Ares and the sacred grove of that god, where the serpent was keeping watch and ward over the fleece as it hung on the leafy branches of an oak. And Aeson's son himself from a golden goblet poured into the river libations of honey and pure wine to Earth and to the gods of the country, and to the souls of dead heroes; and he besought them of their grace to give kindly aid, and to welcome their ship's hawsers with favourable omen. And straightway Ancaeus spake these words:

"We have reached the Colchian land and the stream of Phasis; and it is time for us to take counsel whether we shall make trial of Aeetes with soft words, or an attempt of another kind shall be fitting."

Thus he spake, and by the advice of Argus Jason bade them enter a shaded backwater and let the ship ride at anchor off shore; and it was near at hand in their course and there they passed the night. And soon the dawn appeared to their expectant eyes.

Book III

Come now, Erato, stand by my side, and say next how Jason brought back the fleece to Iolcus aided by the love of Medea. For thou sharest the power of Cypris, and by thy love-cares dost charm unwedded maidens; wherefore to thee too is attached a name that tells of love.

Thus the heroes, unobserved, were waiting in ambush amid the thick reed-beds; but Hera and Athena took note of them, and, apart from Zeus and the other immortals, entered a chamber and took counsel together; and Hera first made trial of Athena:

"Do thou now first, daughter of Zeus, give advice. What must be done? Wilt thou devise some scheme whereby they may seize the golden fleece of Aeetes and bear it to Hellas, or can they deceive the king with soft words and so work persuasion? Of a truth he is terribly overweening. Still it is right to shrink from no endeavour."

Thus she spake, and at once Athena addressed her: "I too was pondering such thoughts in my heart, Hera, when thou didst ask me outright. But not yet do I think that I have conceived a scheme to aid the courage of the heroes, though I have balanced many plans."

She ended, and the goddesses fixed their eyes on the ground at their feet, brooding apart; and straightway Hera was the first to speak her thought: "Come, let us go to Cypris; let both of us accost her and urge her to bid her son (if only he will obey) speed his shaft at the daughter of Aeetes, the enchantress, and charm her with love for Jason. And I deem that by her device he will bring back the fleece to Hellas."

Thus she spake, and the prudent plan pleased Athena, and she addressed her in reply with gentle words:

"Hera, my father begat me to be a stranger to the darts of love, nor do I know any charm to work desire. But if the word pleases thee, surely I will follow; but thou must speak when we meet her."

So she said, and starting forth they came to the mighty palace of Cypris, which her husband, the halt-footed god, had built for her when first he brought her from Zeus to be his wife. And entering the court they stood beneath the gallery of the chamber where the goddess prepared the couch of Hephaestus. But he had gone early to his forge and anvils to a broad cavern in a floating island where with the blast of flame he wrought all manner of curious work; and she all alone was sitting within, on an inlaid seat facing the door. And her white shoulders on each side were covered with the mantle of her hair and she was parting it with a golden comb and about to braid up the long tresses; but when she saw the goddesses before her, she stayed and called them within, and rose from her seat and placed them on couches. Then she herself sat down, and with her hands gathered up the locks still uncombed. And smiling she addressed them with crafty words:

"Good friends, what intent, what occasion brings you here after so long? Why have ye come, not too frequent visitors before, chief among goddesses that ye are?"

And to her Hera replied: "Thou dost mock us, but our hearts are stirred with calamity. For already on the river Phasis the son of Aeson moors his ship, he and his comrades in quest of the fleece. For all their sakes we fear terribly (for the task is nigh at hand) but most for Aeson's son. Him will I deliver, though he sail even to Hades to free Ixion below from his brazen chains, as far as strength lies in my limbs, so that Pelias may not mock at having escaped an evil doom—Pelias who left me unhonoured with sacrifice. Moreover Jason was greatly loved by me before, ever since at the mouth of Anaurus in flood, as I was making trial of men's righteousness, he met me on his return from the chase; and all the mountains and long ridged peaks were sprinkled with snow, and from them the torrents rolling down were rushing with a roar. And he took pity on me in the likeness of an old crone, and raising me on his shoulders himself bore me through the headlong tide. So he is honoured by me unceasingly; nor will Pelias pay the penalty of his outrage, unless thou wilt grant Jason his return."

Thus she spake, and speechlessness seized Cypris. And beholding Hera supplicating her she felt awe, and then addressed her with friendly words: "Dread goddess, may no viler thing than Cypris ever be found, if I disregard thy eager desire in word or deed, whatever my weak arms can effect; and let there be no favour in return."

She spake, and Hera again addressed her with prudence: "It is not in need of might or of strength that we have come. But just quietly bid thy boy charm Aeetes' daughter with love for Jason. For if she will aid him with her kindly counsel, easily do I think he will win the fleece of gold and return to Iolcus, for she is full of wiles."

Thus she spake, and Cypris addressed them both: "Hera and Athena, he will obey you rather than me. For unabashed though he is, there will be some slight shame in his eyes before you: but he has no respect for me, but ever slights me in contentious mood. And, overborne by his naughtiness, I purpose to break his ill-sounding arrows and his bow in his very sight. For in his anger he has threatened that if I shall not keep my hands off him while he still masters his temper, I shall have cause to blame myself thereafter."

So she spake, and the goddesses smiled and looked at each other. But Cypris again spoke, vexed at heart: "To others my sorrows are a jest; nor ought I to tell them to all; I know them too well myself. But now, since this pleases you both, I will make the attempt and coax him, and he will not say me nay."

Thus she spake, and Hera took her slender hand and gently smiling, replied: "Perform this task, Cytherea, straightway, as thou sayest; and be not angry or contend with thy boy; he will cease hereafter to vex thee."

She spake, and left her seat, and Athena accompanied her and they went forth both hastening back. And Cypris went on her way through the glens of Olympus to find her boy. And she found him apart, in the blooming orchard of Zeus, not alone, but with him Ganymedes, whom once Zeus had set to dwell among the immortal gods, being enamoured of his beauty. And they were playing for golden dice, as boys in one house are wont to do. And already greedy Eros was holding the palm of his left hand quite full of them under his breast, standing upright; and on the bloom of his cheeks a sweet blush was glowing. But the other sat crouching hard by, silent and downcast, and he had two dice left which he threw one after the other, and was angered by the loud laughter of Eros. And lo, losing them straightway with the former, he went off empty-handed, helpless, and noticed not the approach of Cypris. And she stood before her boy, and laying her hand on his lips, addressed him:

"Why dost thou smile in triumph, unutterable rogue? Hast thou cheated him thus, and unjustly overcome the innocent child? Come, be ready to perform for me the task I will tell thee of, and I will give thee Zeus' all-beauteous plaything—the one which his dear nurse Adrasteia made for him, while he still lived a child, with childish ways, in the Idaean cave—a well-rounded ball; no better toy wilt thou get from the hands of Hephaestus. All of gold are its zones, and round each double seams run in a circle; but the stitches are hidden, and a dark blue spiral overlays them all. But if thou shouldst cast it with thy hands, lo, like a star, it sends a flaming track through the sky. This I will give thee; and do thou strike with thy shaft and charm the daughter of Aeetes with love for Jason; and let there be no loitering. For then my thanks would be the slighter."

Thus she spake, and welcome were her words to the listening boy. And he threw down all his toys, and eagerly seizing her robe on this side and on that, clung to the goddess. And he implored her to bestow the gift at once; but she, facing him with kindly words, touched his cheeks, kissed him and drew him to her, and replied with a smile:

"Be witness now thy dear head and mine, that surely I will give thee the gift and deceive thee not, if thou wilt strike with thy shaft Aeetes' daughter."

She spoke, and he gathered up his dice, and having well counted them all threw them into his mother's gleaming lap. And straightway with golden baldric he slung round him his quiver from where it leant against a tree-trunk, and took up his curved bow. And he fared forth through the fruitful orchard of the palace of Zeus. Then he passed through the gates of Olympus high in air; hence is a downward path from heaven; and the twin poles rear aloft steep mountain tops—the highest crests of earth, where the risen sun grows ruddy with his first beams. And beneath him there appeared now the life-giving earth and cities of men and sacred streams of rivers, and now in turn mountain peaks and the ocean all around, as he swept through the vast expanse of air.

Now the heroes apart in ambush, in a back-water of the river, were met in council, sitting on the benches of their ship. And Aeson's son himself was speaking among them; and they were listening silently in their places sitting row upon row: "My friends, what pleases myself that will I say out; it is for you to bring about its fulfilment. For in common is our task, and common to all alike is the right of speech; and he who in silence withholds his thought and his counsel, let him know that it is he alone that bereaves this band of its home-return. Do ye others rest here in the ship quietly with your arms; but I will go to the palace of Aeetes, taking with me the sons of Phrixus and two comrades as well. And when I meet him I will first make trial with words to see if he will be willing to give up the golden fleece for friendship's sake or not, but trusting to his might will set at nought our quest. For so, learning his frowardness first from himself, we will consider whether we shall meet him in battle, or some other plan shall avail us, if we refrain from the war-cry. And let us not merely by force, before putting words to the test, deprive him of his own possession. But first it is better to go to him and win his favour by speech. Oftentimes, I ween, does speech accomplish at need what prowess could hardly carry through, smoothing the path in manner befitting. And he once welcomed noble Phrixus, a fugitive from his stepmother's wiles and the sacrifice prepared by his father. For all men everywhere, even the most shameless, reverence the ordinance of Zeus, god of strangers, and regard it."

Thus he spake, and the youths approved the words of Aeson's son with one accord, nor was there one to counsel otherwise. And then he summoned to go with him the sons of Phrixus, and Telamon and Augeias; and himself took Hermes' wand; and at once they passed forth from the ship beyond the reeds and the water to dry land, towards the rising ground of the plain. The plain, I wis, is called Circe's; and here in line grow many willows and osiers, on whose topmost branches hang corpses bound with cords. For even now it is an abomination with the Colchians to burn dead men with fire; nor is it lawful to place them in the earth and raise a mound above, but to wrap them in untanned oxhides and suspend them from trees far from the city. And so earth has an equal portion with air, seeing that they bury the women; for that is the custom of their land.

And as they went Hera with friendly thought spread a thick mist through the city, that they might fare to the palace of Aeetes unseen by the countless hosts of the Colchians. But soon when from the plain they came to the city and Aeetes' palace, then again Hera dispersed the mist. And they stood at the entrance, marvelling at the king's courts and the wide gates and columns which rose in ordered lines round the walls; and high up on the palace a coping of stone rested on brazen triglyphs. And silently they crossed the threshold. And close by garden vines covered with green foliage were in full bloom, lifted high in air. And beneath them ran four fountains, ever-flowing, which Hephaestus had delved out. One was gushing with milk, one with wine, while the third flowed with fragrant oil; and the fourth ran with water, which grew warm at the setting of the Pleiads, and in turn at their rising bubbled forth from the hollow rock, cold as crystal. Such then were the wondrous works that the craftsman-god Hephaestus had fashioned in the palace of Cytaean Aeetes. And he wrought for him bulls with feet of bronze, and their mouths were of bronze, and from them they breathed out a terrible flame of fire; moreover he forged a plough of unbending adamant, all in one piece, in payment of thanks to Helios, who had taken the god up in his chariot when faint from the Phlegraean fight.[22] And here an inner-court was built, and round it were many

---

22. i.e. the fight between the gods and the giants.

well-fitted doors and chambers here and there, and all along on each side was a richly-wrought gallery. And on both sides loftier buildings stood obliquely. In one, which was the loftiest, lordly Aeetes dwelt with his queen; and in another dwelt Apsyrtus, son of Aeetes, whom a Caucasian nymph, Asterodeia, bare before he made Eidyia his wedded wife, the youngest daughter of Tethys and Oceanus. And the sons of the Colchians called him by the new name of Phaëthon,[23] because he outshone all the youths. The other buildings the handmaidens had, and the two daughters of Aeetes, Chalciope and Medea. Medea then [they found] going from chamber to chamber in search of her sister, for Hera detained her within that day; but beforetime she was not wont to haunt the palace, but all day long was busied in Hecate's temple, since she herself was the priestess of the goddess. And when she saw them she cried aloud, and quickly Chalciope caught the sound; and her maids, throwing down at their feet their yarn and their thread, rushed forth all in a throng. And she, beholding her sons among them, raised her hands aloft through joy; and so they likewise greeted their mother, and when they saw her embraced her in their gladness; and she with many sobs spoke thus:

"After all then, ye were not destined to leave me in your heedlessness and to wander far; but fate has turned you back. Poor wretch that I am! What a yearning for Hellas from some woeful madness seized you at the behest of your father Phrixus. Bitter sorrows for my heart did he ordain when dying. And why should ye go to the city of Orchomenus, whoever this Orchomenus is, for the sake of Athamas' wealth, leaving your mother alone to bear her grief?"

Such were her words; and Aeetes came forth last of all and Eidyia herself came, the queen of Aeetes, on hearing the voice of Chalciope; and straightway all the court was filled with a throng. Some of the thralls were busied with a mighty bull, others with the axe were cleaving dry billets, and others heating with fire water for the baths; nor was there one who relaxed his toil, serving the king.

Meantime Eros passed unseen through the grey mist, causing confusion, as when against grazing heifers rises the gadfly, which oxherds call the breese. And quickly beneath the lintel in the porch he strung his bow and took from the quiver an arrow unshot before, messenger of pain. And with swift feet unmarked he passed the threshold and

---

23. i.e. the Shining One.

APOLLONIUS OF RHODES

keenly glanced around; and gliding close by Aeson's son he laid the arrow-notch on the cord in the centre, and drawing wide apart with both hands he shot at Medea; and speechless amazement seized her soul. But the god himself flashed back again from the high-roofed hall, laughing loud; and the bolt burnt deep down in the maiden's heart, like a flame; and ever she kept darting bright glances straight up at Aeson's son, and within her breast her heart panted fast through anguish, all remembrance left her, and her soul melted with the sweet pain. And as a poor woman heaps dry twigs round a blazing brand—a daughter of toil, whose task is the spinning of wool, that she may kindle a blaze at night beneath her roof, when she has waked very early—and the flame waxing wondrous great from the small brand consumes all the twigs together; so, coiling round her heart, burnt secretly Love the destroyer; and the hue of her soft cheeks went and came, now pale, now red, in her soul's distraction.

Now when the thralls had laid a banquet ready before them, and they had refreshed themselves with warm baths, gladly did they please their souls with meat and drink. And thereafter Aeetes questioned the sons of his daughter, addressing them with these words:

"Sons of my daughter and of Phrixus, whom beyond all strangers I honoured in my halls, how have ye come returning back to Aea? Did some calamity cut short your escape in the midst? Ye did not listen when I set before you the boundless length of the way. For I marked it once, whirled along in the chariot of my father Helios, when he was bringing my sister Circe to the western land and we came to the shore of the Tyrrhenian mainland, where even now she abides, exceeding far from Colchis. But what pleasure is there in words? Do ye tell me plainly what has been your fortune, and who these men are, your companions, and where from your hollow ship ye came ashore."

Such were his questions, and Argus, before all his brethren, being fearful for the mission of Aeson's son, gently replied, for he was the elder-born:

"Aeetes, that ship forthwith stormy blasts tore asunder, and ourselves, crouching on the beams, a wave drove on to the beach of the isle of Enyalius[24] in the murky night; and some god preserved us. For even the birds of Ares that haunted the desert isle beforetime, not even them did we find. But these men had driven them off, having landed from

---

24. A name of Ares.

their ship on the day before; and the will of Zeus taking pity on us, or some fate, detained them there, since they straightway gave us both food and clothing in abundance, when they heard the illustrious name of Phrixus and thine own; for to thy city are they faring. And if thou dost wish to know their errand, I will not hide it from thee. A certain king, vehemently longing to drive this man far from his fatherland and possessions, because in might he outshone all the sons of Aeolus, sends him to voyage hither on a bootless venture; and asserts that the stock of Aeolus will not escape the heart-grieving wrath and rage of implacable Zeus, nor the unbearable curse and vengeance due for Phrixus, until the fleece comes back to Hellas. And their ship was fashioned by Pallas Athena, not such a one as are the ships among the Colchians, on the vilest of which we chanced. For the fierce waves and wind broke her utterly to pieces; but the other holds firm with her bolts, even though all the blasts should buffet her. And with equal swiftness she speedeth before the wind and when the crew ply the oar with unresting hands. And he hath gathered in her the mightiest heroes of all Achaea, and hath come to thy city from wandering far through cities and gulfs of the dread ocean, in the hope that thou wilt grant him the fleece. But as thou dost please, so shall it be, for he cometh not to use force, but is eager to pay thee a recompense for the gift. He has heard from me of thy bitter foes the Sauromatae, and he will subdue them to thy sway. And if thou desirest to know their names and lineage I will tell thee all. This man on whose account the rest were gathered from Hellas, they call Jason, son of Aeson, whom Cretheus begat. And if in truth he is of the stock of Cretheus himself, thus he would be our kinsman on the father's side. For Cretheus and Athamas were both sons of Aeolus; and Phrixus was the son of Athamas, son of Aeolus. And here, if thou hast heard at all of the seed of Helios, thou dost behold Augeias; and this is Telamon sprung from famous Aeacus; and Zeus himself begat Aeacus. And so all the rest, all the comrades that follow him, are the sons or grandsons of the immortals."

Such was the tale of Argus; but the king at his words was filled with rage as he heard; and his heart was lifted high in wrath. And he spake in heavy displeasure; and was angered most of all with the son of Chalciope; for he deemed that on their account the strangers had come; and in his fury his eyes flashed forth beneath his brows:

"Begone from my sight, felons, straightway, ye and your tricks, from the land, ere someone see a fleece and a Phrixus to his sorrow. Banded together with your friends from Hellas, not for the fleece, but to seize my sceptre and royal power have ye come hither. Had ye not first tasted of my table, surely would I have cut out your tongues and hewn off both hands and sent you forth with your feet alone, so that ye might be stayed from starting hereafter. And what lies have ye uttered against the blessed gods!"

Thus he spake in his wrath; and mightily from its depths swelled the heart of Aeacus' son, and his soul within longed to speak a deadly word in defiance, but Aeson's son checked him, for he himself first made gentle answer:

"Aeetes, bear with this armed band, I pray. For not in the way thou deemest have we come to thy city and palace, no, nor yet with such desires. For who would of his own will dare to cross so wide a sea for the goods of a stranger? But fate and the ruthless command of a presumptuous king urged me. Grant a favour to thy suppliants, and to all Hellas will I publish a glorious fame of thee; yea, we are ready now to pay thee a swift recompense in war, whether it be the Sauromatae or some other people that thou art eager to subdue to thy sway."

He spake, flattering him with gentle utterance; but the king's soul brooded a twofold purpose within him, whether he should attack and slay them on the spot or should make trial of their might. And this, as he pondered, seemed the better way, and he addressed Jason in answer:

"Stranger, why needest thou go through thy tale to the end? For if ye are in truth of heavenly race, or have come in no wise inferior to me, to win the goods of strangers, I will give thee the fleece to bear away, if thou dost wish, when I have tried thee. For against brave men I bear no grudge, such as ye yourselves tell me of him who bears sway in Hellas. And the trial of your courage and might shall be a contest which I myself can compass with my hands, deadly though it be. Two bulls with feet of bronze I have that pasture on the plain of Ares, breathing forth flame from their jaws; them do I yoke and drive over the stubborn field of Ares, four plough-gates; and quickly cleaving it with the share up to the headland, I cast into the furrows for seed, not the corn of Demeter, but the teeth of a dread serpent that grow up into the fashion of armed men; them I slay at once, cutting them down beneath my spear as they rise against me on all sides. In the morning do I yoke the oxen, and at eventide I cease from the harvesting. And thou, if thou wilt accomplish such deeds as these, on that very day shalt carry off the fleece to the king's palace; ere that time comes I will not give it, expect it not. For indeed it is unseemly that a brave man should yield to a coward."

Thus he spake; and Jason, fixing his eyes on the ground, sat just as he was, speechless, helpless in his evil plight. For a long time he turned the matter this way and that, and could in no way take on him the task with courage, for a mighty task it seemed; and at last he made reply with crafty words:

"With thy plea of right, Aeetes, thou dost shut me in overmuch. Wherefore also I will dare that contest, monstrous as it is, though it be my doom to die. For nothing will fall upon men more dread than dire necessity, which indeed constrained me to come hither at a king's command."

Thus he spake, smitten by his helpless plight; and the king with grim words addressed him, sore troubled as he was: "Go forth now to the gathering, since thou art eager for the toil; but if thou shouldst fear to lift the yoke upon the oxen or shrink from the deadly harvesting, then all this shall be my care, so that another too may shudder to come to a man that is better than he."

He spake outright; and Jason rose from his seat, and Augeias and Telamon at once; and Argus followed alone, for he signed to his brothers to stay there on the spot meantime; and so they went forth from the hall. And wonderfully among them all shone the son of Aeson for beauty and grace; and the maiden looked at him with stealthy glance, holding her bright veil aside, her heart smouldering with pain; and her soul creeping like a dream flitted in his track as he went. So they passed forth from the palace sorely troubled. And Chalciope, shielding herself from the wrath of Aeetes, had gone quickly to her chamber with her sons. And Medea likewise followed, and much she brooded in her soul all the cares that the Loves awaken. And before her eyes the vision still appeared—himself what like he was, with what vesture he was clad, what things he spake, how he sat on his seat, how he moved forth to the door—and as she pondered she deemed there never was such another man; and ever in her ears rung his voice and the honey-sweet words which he uttered. And she feared for him, lest the oxen or Aeetes with his own hand should slay him; and she mourned him as though already slain outright, and in her affliction a round tear through very grievous pity coursed down her cheek: and gently weeping she lifted up her voice aloud:

"Why does this grief come upon me, poor wretch? Whether he be the best of heroes now about to perish, or the worst, let him go to his doom. Yet I would that he had escaped unharmed; yea, may this be so, revered goddess, daughter of Perses, may he avoid death and return home; but if it be his lot to be o'ermastered by the oxen, may he first learn this that I at least do not rejoice in his cruel calamity."

Thus then was the maiden's heart racked by love-cares. But when the others had gone forth from the people and the city, along the path by which at the first they had come from the plain, then Argus addressed Jason with these words:

"Son of Aeson, thou wilt despise the counsel which I will tell thee, but, though in evil plight, it is not fitting to forbear from the trial. Ere now thou hast heard me tell of a maiden that uses sorcery under the guidance of Hecate, Perses' daughter. If we could win her aid there will be no dread, methinks, of thy defeat in the contest; but terribly do I fear that my mother will not take this task upon her. Nevertheless I will go back again to entreat her, for a common destruction overhangs us all."

He spake with goodwill, and Jason answered with these words: "Good friend, if this is good in thy sight, I say not nay. Go and move thy mother, beseeching her aid with prudent words; pitiful indeed is our hope when we have put our return in the keeping of women." So he spake, and quickly they reached the back-water. And their comrades joyfully questioned them, when they saw them close at hand; and to them spoke Aeson's son grieved at heart:

"My friends, the heart of ruthless Aeetes is utterly filled with wrath against us, for not at all can the goal be reached either by me or by you who question me. He said that two bulls with feet of bronze pasture on the plain of Ares, breathing forth flame from their jaws. And with these he bade me plough the field, four plough-gates; and said that he would give me from a serpent's jaws seed which will raise up earthborn men in armour of bronze; and on the same day I must slay them. This task—for there was nothing better to devise—I took on myself outright."

Thus he spake; and to all the contest seemed one that none could accomplish, and long, quiet and silent, they looked at one another, bowed down with the calamity and their despair; but at last Peleus spake with courageous words among all the chiefs: "It is time to be counselling what we shall do. Yet there is not so much profit, I trow, in counsel as in the might of our hands. If thou then, hero son of Aeson, art minded to yoke Aeetes' oxen, and art eager for the toil, surely thou wilt keep thy promise and make thyself ready. But if thy soul trusts not her prowess utterly, then neither bestir thyself nor sit still and look round for some one else of these men. For it is not I who will flinch, since the bitterest pain will be but death."

So spake the son of Aeacus; and Telamon's soul was stirred, and quickly he started up in eagerness; and Idas rose up the third in his pride; and the twin sons of Tyndareus; and with them Oeneus' son who was numbered among strong men, though even the soft down on his cheek showed not yet; with such courage was his soul uplifted. But the others gave way to these in silence. And straightway Argus spake these words to those that longed for the contest:

"My friends, this indeed is left us at the last. But I deem that there will come to you some timely aid from my mother. Wherefore, eager though ye be, refrain and abide in your ship a little longer as before, for it is better to forbear than recklessly to choose an evil fate. There is a maiden, nurtured in the halls of Aeetes, whom the goddess Hecate taught to handle magic herbs with exceeding skill—all that the land and flowing waters produce. With them is quenched the blast of unwearied flame, and at once she stays the course of rivers as they rush roaring on, and checks the stars and the paths of the sacred moon. Of her we bethought us as we came hither along the path from the palace, if haply my mother, her own sister, might persuade her to aid us in the venture. And if this is pleasing to you as well, surely on this very day will I return to the palace of Aeetes to make trial; and perchance with some god's help shall I make the trial."

Thus he spake, and the gods in their goodwill gave them a sign. A trembling dove in her flight from a mighty hawk fell from on high, terrified, into the lap of Aeson's son, and the hawk fell impaled on the stern-ornament. And quickly Mopsus with prophetic words spake among them all:

"For you, friends, this sign has been wrought by the will of heaven; in no other way is it possible to interpret its meaning better, than to seek out the maiden and entreat her with manifold skill. And I think she will not reject our prayer, if in truth Phineus said that our return should be with the help of the Cyprian goddess. It was her gentle bird that escaped death; and as my heart within me foresees according to this omen, so may it prove! But, my friends, let us call on Cytherea to aid us, and now at once obey the counsels of Argus."

He spake, and the warriors approved, remembering the injunctions of Phineus; but all alone leapt up Aphareian Idas and shouted loudly in terrible wrath: "Shame on us, have we come here fellow-voyagers with women, calling on Cypris for help and not on the mighty strength of Enyalius? And do ye look to doves and hawks to save yourselves from contests? Away with you, take thought not for deeds of war, but by supplication to beguile weakling girls."

Such were his eager words; and of his comrades many murmured low, but none uttered a word of answer back. And he sat down in wrath; and at once Jason roused them and uttered his own thought: "Let Argus set forth from the ship, since this pleases all; but we will now move from the river and openly fasten our hawsers to the shore. For surely it is not fitting for us to hide any longer cowering from the battle-cry."

So he spake, and straightway sent Argus to return in haste to the city; and they drew the anchors on board at the command of Aeson's son, and rowed the ship close to the shore, a little away from the back-water.

But straightway Aeetes held an assembly of the Colchians far aloof from his palace at a spot where they sat in times before, to devise against the Minyae grim treachery and troubles. And he threatened that when first the oxen should have torn in pieces the man who had taken upon him to perform the heavy task, he would hew down the oak grove above the wooded hill, and burn the ship and her crew, that so they might vent forth in ruin their grievous insolence, for all their haughty schemes. For never would he have welcomed the Aeolid Phrixus as a guest in his halls, in spite of his sore need, Phrixus, who surpassed all strangers in gentleness and fear of the gods, had not Zeus himself sent Hermes his messenger down from heaven, so that he might meet with a friendly host; much less would pirates coming to his land be let go scatheless for long, men whose care it was to lift their hands and seize the goods of others, and to weave secret webs of guile, and harry the steadings of herdsmen with ill-sounding forays. And he said that besides all that the sons of Phrixus should pay a fitting penalty to himself for returning in consort with evil-doers, that they might recklessly drive him from his honour and his throne; for once he had heard a baleful prophecy from his father Helios, that he must avoid the secret treachery and schemes of his own offspring and their crafty mischief. Wherefore he was sending them, as they desired, to the Achaean land at the bidding of their father—a long journey. Nor had he ever so slight a fear of his daughters, that they would form some hateful scheme, nor of his son Apsyrtus; but this curse was being fulfilled in the children of Chalciope. And he proclaimed terrible things in his rage against the strangers, and loudly threatened to keep watch over the ship and its crew, so that no one might escape calamity.

Meantime Argus, going to Aeetes' palace, with manifold pleading besought his mother to pray Medea's aid; and Chalciope herself already had the same thoughts, but fear checked her soul lest haply either fate should withstand and she should entreat her in vain, all distraught as she would be at her father's deadly wrath, or, if Medea yielded to her prayers, her deeds should be laid bare and open to view.

Now a deep slumber had relieved the maiden from her love-pains as she lay upon her couch. But straightway fearful dreams, deceitful, such as trouble one in grief, assailed her. And she thought that the stranger had taken on him the contest, not because he longed to win the ram's fleece, and that he had not come on that account to Aeetes' city, but to lead her away, his wedded wife, to his own home; and she dreamed that herself contended with the oxen and wrought the task with exceeding ease; and that her own parents set at naught their promise, for it was not the maiden they had challenged to yoke the oxen but the stranger himself; from that arose a contention of doubtful issue between her father and the strangers; and both laid the decision upon her, to be as she should direct in her mind. But she suddenly, neglecting her parents, chose the stranger. And measureless anguish seized them and they shouted out in their wrath; and with the cry sleep released its hold upon her. Quivering with fear she started up, and stared round the walls of her chamber, and with difficulty did she gather her spirit within her as before, and lifted her voice aloud:

"Poor wretch, how have gloomy dreams affrighted me! I fear that this voyage of the heroes will bring some great evil. My heart is trembling for the stranger. Let him woo some Achaean girl fair away among his own folk; let maidenhood be mine and the home of my parents. Yet, taking to myself a reckless heart, I will no more keep aloof but will make trial of my sister to see if she will entreat me to aid in the contest, through grief for her own sons; this would quench the bitter pain in my heart."

She spake, and rising from her bed opened the door of her chamber, bare-footed, clad in one robe; and verily she desired to go to her sister, and crossed the threshold. And for long she stayed there at the entrance of her chamber, held back by shame; and she turned back once more; and again she came forth from within, and again stole back; and idly did her feet bear her this way and that; yea, as oft as she went straight on, shame held her within the chamber, and though held back by shame, bold desire kept urging her on. Thrice she made the attempt and thrice she checked herself, the fourth time she fell on her bed face downward writhing in pain. And as when a bride in her chamber bewails her youthful husband, to whom her brothers and parents have given her, nor yet does she hold converse with all her attendants for shame and for thinking of him; but she sits apart in her grief; and some doom has destroyed him, before they have had pleasure of each other's charms; and she with heart on fire silently weeps, beholding her widowed couch, in fear lest the women should mock and revile her: like, to her did Medea lament. And suddenly as she was in the midst of her tears, one of the handmaids came forth and noticed her, one who was her youthful attendant; and straightway she told Chalciope, who sat in the midst of her sons devising how to win over her sister. And when Chalciope heard the strange tale from the handmaid, not even so did she disregard it. And she rushed in dismay from her chamber right on to the chamber where the maiden lay in her anguish, having torn her cheeks on each side; and when Chalciope saw her eyes all dimmed with tears, she thus addressed her:

"Ah me, Medea, why dost thou weep so? What hath befallen thee? What terrible grief has entered thy heart? Has some heaven-sent disease enwrapt thy frame, or hast thou heard from our father some deadly threat concerning me and my sons? Would that I did not behold this home of my parents, or the city, but dwelt at the ends of the earth, where not even the name of Colchians is known!"

Thus she spake, and her sister's cheeks flushed; and though she was eager to reply, long did maiden shame restrain her. At one moment the word rose on the end of her tongue, at another it fluttered back deep within her breast. And often through her lovely lips it strove for utterance; but no sound came forth; till at last she spoke with guileful words; for the bold Loves were pressing her hard:

"Chalciope, my heart is all trembling for thy sons, lest my father forthwith destroy them together with the strangers. Slumbering just now in a short-lived sleep such a ghastly dream did I see—may some god forbid its fulfilment and never mayst thou win for thyself bitter care on thy sons' account."

She spake, making trial of her sister to see if she first would entreat help for her sons. And utterly unbearable grief surged over Chalciope's soul for fear at what she heard; and then she replied: "Yea, I myself too have come to thee in eager furtherance of this purpose, if thou wouldst haply devise with me and prepare some help. But swear by Earth and

Heaven that thou wilt keep secret in thy heart what I shall tell thee, and be fellow-worker with me. I implore thee by the blessed gods, by thyself and by thy parents, not to see them destroyed by an evil doom piteously; or else may I die with my dear sons and come back hereafter from Hades an avenging Fury to haunt thee."

Thus she spake, and straightway a torrent of tears gushed forth, and low down she clasped her sister's knees with both hands and let her head sink on to her breast. Then they both made piteous lamentation over each other, and through the halls rose the faint sound of women weeping in anguish. Medea, sore troubled, first addressed her sister:

"God help thee, what healing can I bring thee for what thou speakest of, horrible curses and Furies? Would that it were firmly in my power to save thy sons! Be witness that mighty oath of the Colchians by which thou urgest me to swear, the great Heaven, and Earth beneath, mother of the gods, that as far as strength lies in me, never shalt thou fail of help, if only thy prayers can be accomplished."

She spake, and Chalciope thus replied: "Couldst thou not then, for the stranger—who himself craves thy aid—devise some trick or some wise thought to win the contest, for the sake of my sons? And from him has come Argus urging me to try to win thy help; I left him in the palace meantime while I came hither."

Thus she spake, and Medea's heart bounded with joy within her, and at once her fair cheeks flushed, and a mist swam before her melting eyes, and she spake as follows: "Chalciope, as is dear and delightful to thee and thy sons, even so will I do. Never may the dawn appear again to my eyes, never mayst thou see me living any longer, if I should take thought for anything before thy life or thy sons' lives, for they are my brothers, my dear kinsmen and youthful companions. So do I declare myself to be thy sister, and thy daughter too, for thou didst lift me to thy breast when an infant equally with them, as I ever heard from my mother in past days. But go, bury my kindness in silence, so that I may carry out my promise unknown to my parents; and at dawn I will bring to Hecate's temple charms to cast a spell upon the bulls."

Thus Chalciope went back from the chamber, and made known to her sons the help given by her sister. And again did shame and hateful fear seize Medea thus left alone, that she should devise such deeds for a man in her father's despite.

Then did night draw darkness over the earth; and on the sea sailors from their ships looked towards the Bear and the stars of Orion; and now the wayfarer and the warder longed for sleep, and the pall of slumber wrapped round the mother whose children were dead; nor was there any more the barking of dogs through the city, nor sound of men's voices; but silence held the blackening gloom. But not indeed upon Medea came sweet sleep. For in her love for Aeson's son many cares kept her wakeful, and she dreaded the mighty strength of the bulls, beneath whose fury he was like to perish by an unseemly fate in the field of Ares. And fast did her heart throb within her breast, as a sunbeam quivers upon the walls of a house when flung up from water, which is just poured forth in a caldron or a pail may be; and hither and thither on the swift eddy does it dart and dance along; even so the maiden's heart quivered in her breast. And the tear of pity flowed from her eyes, and ever within anguish tortured her, a smouldering fire through her frame, and about her fine nerves and deep down beneath the nape of the neck where the pain enters keenest, whenever the unwearied Loves direct against the heart their shafts of agony. And she thought now that she would give him the charms to cast a spell on the bulls, now that she would not, and that she herself would perish; and again that she would not perish and would not give the charms, but just as she was would endure her fate in silence. Then sitting down she wavered in mind and said:

"Poor wretch, must I toss hither and thither in woe? On every side my heart is in despair; nor is there any help for my pain; but it burneth ever thus. Would that I had been slain by the swift shafts of Artemis before I had set eyes on him, before Chalciope's sons reached the Achaean land. Some god or some Fury brought them hither for our grief, a cause of many tears. Let him perish in the contest if it be his lot to die in the field. For how could I prepare the charms without my parents' knowledge? What story can I tell them? What trick, what cunning device for aid can I find? If I see him alone, apart from his comrades, shall I greet him? Ill-starred that I am! I cannot hope that I should rest from my sorrows even though he perished; then will evil come to me when he is bereft of life. Perish all shame, perish all glory; may he, saved by my effort, go scatheless wherever his heart desires. But as for me, on the day when he bides the contest in triumph, may I die either straining my neck in the noose from the roof-tree or tasting drugs destructive of life. But even so, when I am dead, they will fling out taunts against me; and every city far away will ring with my doom, and the Colchian women, tossing my name on their lips hither and thither, will revile me with unseemly mocking—the maid who cared so much for a stranger that she died, the maid who disgraced her home and her parents, yielding to a mad passion. And what disgrace will not be mine? Alas for my infatuation! Far better would it be for me to forsake life this very night in my chamber by some mysterious fate, escaping all slanderous reproach, before I complete such nameless dishonour."

She spake, and brought a casket wherein lay many drugs, some for healing, others for killing, and placing it upon her knees she wept. And she drenched her bosom with ceaseless tears, which flowed in torrents as she sat, bitterly bewailing her own fate. And she longed to choose a murderous drug to taste it, and now she was loosening the bands of the casket eager to take it forth, unhappy maid! But suddenly a deadly fear of hateful Hades came upon her heart. And long she held back in speechless horror, and all around her thronged visions of the pleasing cares of life. She thought of all the delightful things that are among the living, she thought of her joyous playmates, as a maiden will; and the sun grew sweeter than ever to behold, seeing that in truth her soul yearned for all. And she put the casket again from off her knees, all changed by the prompting of Hera, and no more did she waver in purpose; but longed for the rising dawn to appear quickly, that she might give him the charms to work the spell as she had promised, and meet him face to face. And often did she loosen the bolts of her door, to watch for the faint gleam: and welcome to her did the dayspring shed its light, and folk began to stir throughout the city.

Then Argus bade his brothers remain there to learn the maiden's mind and plans, but himself turned back and went to the ship.

Now soon as ever the maiden saw the light of dawn, with her hands she gathered up her golden tresses which were floating round her shoulders in careless disarray, and bathed her tear-stained cheeks, and made her skin shine with ointment sweet as nectar; and she donned a beautiful robe, fitted with well-bent clasps, and above on her head, divinely fair, she threw a veil gleaming like silver. And there, moving to and fro in the palace, she trod the ground forgetful of the heaven-sent woes thronging round her and of others that were destined to follow. And she called to her maids. Twelve they were, who lay during the night in the vestibule of her fragrant chamber, young as herself, not yet sharing the bridal couch, and she bade them hastily yoke the mules to the chariot to bear her to the beauteous shrine of Hecate. Thereupon the handmaids were making ready the chariot; and Medea meanwhile took from the hollow casket a charm which men say is called the charm of Prometheus. If a man should anoint his body therewithal, having first appeased the Maiden, the only-begotten, with sacrifice by night, surely that man could not be wounded by the stroke of bronze nor would he flinch from blazing fire; but for that day he would prove superior both in prowess and in might. It shot up first-born when the ravening eagle on the rugged flanks of Caucasus let drip to the earth the blood-like ichor[25] of tortured Prometheus. And its flower appeared a cubit above ground in colour like the Corycian crocus, rising on twin stalks; but in the earth the root was like newly-cut flesh. The dark juice of it, like the sap of a mountain-oak, she had gathered in a Caspian shell to make the charm withal, when she had first bathed in seven ever-flowing streams, and had called seven times on Brimo, nurse of youth, night-wandering Brimo, of the underworld, queen among the dead,—in the gloom of night, clad in dusky garments. And beneath, the dark earth shook and bellowed when the Titanian root was cut; and the son of Iapetus himself groaned, his soul distraught with pain. And she brought the charm forth and placed it in the fragrant band which engirdled her, just beneath her bosom, divinely fair. And going forth she mounted the swift chariot, and with her went two handmaidens on each side. And she herself took the reins and in her right hand the well-fashioned whip, and drove through the city; and the rest, the handmaids, laid their hands on the chariot behind and ran along the broad highway; and they kilted up their light robes above their white knees. And even as by the mild waters of Parthenius, or after bathing in the river Amnisus, Leto's daughter stands upon her golden chariot and courses over the hills with her swift-footed roes, to greet from afar some richly-steaming hecatomb; and with her come the nymphs in attendance, gathering, some at the spring of Amnisus itself, others by the glens and many-fountained peaks; and round her whine and fawn the beasts cowering as she moves along: thus they sped through the city; and on both sides the people gave way shunning the eyes of the royal maiden. But when she had left the city's well paved streets, and was approaching the shrine as she drove over the plains, then she alighted eagerly from the smooth-running chariot and spake as follows among her maidens:

"Friends, verily have I sinned greatly and took no heed not to go among the stranger-folk[26] who roam over our land. The whole city is

---

25. i.e. the liquid that flows in the veins of gods.
26. Or, reading, "took no heed of the cause of wrath with the stranger-folk"

smitten with dismay; wherefore no one of the women who formerly gathered here day by day has now come hither. But since we have come and no one else draws near, come, let us satisfy our souls without stint with soothing song, and when we have plucked the fair flowers amid the tender grass, that very hour will we return. And with many a gift shall ye reach home this very day, if ye will gladden me with this desire of mine. For Argus pleads with me, also Chalciope herself; but this that ye hear from me keep silently in your hearts, lest the tale reach my father's ears. As for yon stranger who took on him the task with the oxen, they bid me receive his gifts and rescue him from the deadly contest. And I approved their counsel, and I have summoned him to come to my presence apart from his comrades, so that we may divide the gifts among ourselves if he bring them in his hands, and in return may give him a baleful charm. But when he comes, do ye stand aloof."

So she spake, and the crafty counsel pleased them all. And straightway Argus drew Aeson's son apart from his comrades as soon as he heard from his brothers that Medea had gone at daybreak to the holy shrine of Hecate, and led him over the plain; and with them went Mopsus, son of Ampycus, skilled to utter oracles from the appearance of birds, and skilled to give good counsel to those who set out on a journey.

Never yet had there been such a man in the days of old, neither of all the heroes of the lineage of Zeus himself, nor of those who sprung from the blood of the other gods, as on that day the bride of Zeus made Jason, both to look upon and to hold converse with. Even his comrades wondered as they gazed upon him, radiant with manifold graces; and the son of Ampycus rejoiced in their journey, already foreboding how all would end.

Now by the path along the plain there stands near the shrine a poplar with its crown of countless leaves, whereon often chattering crows would roost. One of them meantime as she clapped her wings aloft in the brandies uttered the counsels of Hera:

"What a pitiful seer is this, that has not the wit to conceive even what children know, how that no maiden will say a word of sweetness or love to a youth when strangers be near. Begone, sorry prophet, witless one; on thee neither Cypris nor the gentle Loves breathe in their kindness."

She spake chiding, and Mopsus smiled to hear the god-sent voice of the bird, and thus addressed them: "Do thou, son of Aeson, pass on to the temple, where thou wilt find the maiden; and very kind will her greeting be to thee through the prompting of Cypris, who will be thy helpmate in the contest, even as Phineus, Agenor's son, foretold. But we two, Argus and I, will await thy return, apart in this very spot do thou all alone be a suppliant and win her over with prudent words."

He spake wisely, and both at once gave approval. Nor was Medea's heart turned to other thoughts, for all her singing, and never a song that she essayed pleased her long in her sport. But in confusion she ever faltered, nor did she keep her eyes resting quietly upon the throng of her handmaids; but to the paths far off she strained her gaze, turning her face aside. Oft did her heart sink fainting within Tier bosom whenever she fancied she heard passing by the sound of a footfall or of the wind. But soon he appeared to her longing eyes, striding along loftily, like Sirius coming from ocean, which rises fair and clear to see, but brings unspeakable mischief to flocks; thus then did Aeson's son come to her, fair to see, but the sight of him brought love-sick care. Her heart fell from out her bosom, and a dark mist came over her eyes, and a hot blush covered her cheeks. And she had no strength to lift her knees backwards or forwards, but her feet beneath were rooted to the ground; and meantime all her handmaidens had drawn aside. So they two stood face to face without a word, without a sound, like oaks or lofty pines, which stand quietly side by side on the mountains when the wind is still; then again, when stirred by the breath of the wind, they murmur ceaselessly; so they two were destined to tell out all their tale, stirred by the breath of Love. And Aeson's son saw that she had fallen into some heaven-sent calamity, and with soothing words thus addressed her:

"Why, pray, maiden, dost thou fear me so much, all alone as I am? Never was I one of these idle boasters such as other men are—not even aforetime, when I dwelt in my own country. Wherefore, maiden, be not too much abashed before me, either to enquire whatever thou wilt or to speak thy mind. But since we have met one another with friendly hearts, in a hallowed spot, where it is wrong to sin, speak openly and ask questions, and beguile me not with pleasing words, for at the first thou didst promise thy sister to give me the charms my heart desires. I implore thee by Hecate herself, by thy parents, and by Zeus who holds his guardian hand over strangers and suppliants; I come here to thee both a suppliant and a stranger, bending the knee in my sore need. For without thee and thy sister never shall I prevail in the grievous contest. And to thee will I render thanks hereafter for thy aid, as is right and fitting for men who dwell far off, making glorious thy name and fame; and the rest of the heroes, returning to Hellas, will spread thy renown and so will the heroes' wives and mothers, who now perhaps are sitting on the shore and making moan for us; their painful affliction thou mightest scatter to the winds. In days past the maiden Ariadne, daughter of Minos, with kindly intent rescued Theseus from grim contests—the maiden whom Pasiphae daughter of Helios bare. But she, when Minos had lulled his wrath to rest, went aboard the ship with him and left her fatherland; and her even the immortal gods loved, and, as a sign in mid-sky, a crown of stars, which men call Ariadne's crown, rolls along all night among the heavenly constellations. So to thee too shall be thanks from the gods, if thou wilt save so mighty an array of chieftains. For surely from thy lovely form thou art like to excel in gentle courtesy."

Thus he spake, honouring her; and she cast her eyes down with a smile divinely sweet; and her soul melted within her, uplifted by his praise, and she gazed upon him face to face; nor did she know what word to utter first, but was eager to pour out everything at once. And forth from her fragrant girdle ungrudgingly she brought out the charm; and he at once received it in his hands with joy. And she would even have drawn out all her soul from her breast and given it to him, exulting in his desire; so wonderfully did love flash forth a sweet flame from the golden head of Aeson's son; and he captivated her gleaming eyes; and her heart within grew warm, melting away as the dew melts away round roses when warmed by the morning's light. And now both were fixing their eyes on the ground abashed, and again were throwing glances at each other, smiling with the light of love beneath their radiant brows. And at last and scarcely then did the maiden greet him:

"Take heed now, that I may devise help for thee. When at thy coming my father has given thee the deadly teeth from the dragon's jaws for sowing, then watch for the time when the night is parted in twain, then bathe in the stream of the tireless river, and alone, apart from others, clad in dusky raiment, dig a rounded pit; and therein slay a ewe, and sacrifice it whole, heaping high the pyre on the very edge of the pit. And propitiate only-begotten Hecate, daughter of Perses, pouring from a goblet the hive-stored labour of bees. And then, when thou hast heedfully sought the grace of the goddess, retreat from the pyre; and let neither the sound of feet drive thee to turn back, nor the baying of hounds, lest haply thou shouldst maim all the rites and thyself fail to return duly to thy comrades. And at dawn steep this charm in water, strip, and anoint thy

APOLLONIUS OF RHODES

body therewith as with oil; and in it there will be boundless prowess and mighty strength, and thou wilt deem thyself a match not for men but for the immortal gods. And besides, let thy spear and shield and sword be sprinkled. Thereupon the spear-heads of the earthborn men shall not pierce thee, nor the flame of the deadly bulls as it rushes forth resistless. But such thou shalt be not for long, but for that one day; still never flinch from the contest. And I will tell thee besides of yet another help. As soon as thou hast yoked the strong oxen, and with thy might and thy prowess hast ploughed all the stubborn fallow, and now along the furrows the Giants are springing up, when the serpent's teeth are sown on the dusky clods, if thou markest them uprising in throngs from the fallow, cast unseen among them a massy stone; and they over it, like ravening hounds over their food, will slay one another; and do thou thyself hasten to rush to the battle-strife, and the fleece thereupon thou shalt bear far away from Aea; nevertheless, depart wherever thou wilt, or thy pleasure takes thee, when thou hast gone hence."

Thus she spake, and cast her eyes to her feet in silence, and her cheek, divinely fair, was wet with warm tears as she sorrowed for that he was about to wander far from her side over the wide sea: and once again she addressed him face to face with mournful words, and took his right hand; for now shame had left her eyes:

"Remember, if haply thou returnest to thy home, Medea's name; and so will I remember thine, though thou be far away. And of thy kindness tell me this, where is thy home, whither wilt thou sail hence in thy ship over the sea; wilt thou come near wealthy Orchomenus, or near the Aeaean isle? And tell me of the maiden, whosoever she be that thou hast named, the far-renowned daughter of Pasiphae, who is kinswoman to my father."

Thus she spake; and over him too, at the tears of the maiden, stole Love the destroyer, and he thus answered her:

"All too surely do I deem that never by night and never by day will I forget thee if I escape death and indeed make my way in safety to the Achaean land, and Aeetes set not before us some other contest worse than this. And if it pleases thee to know about my fatherland, I will tell it out; for indeed my own heart bids me do that. There is a land encircled by lofty mountains, rich in sheep and in pasture, where Prometheus, son of Iapetus, begat goodly Deucalion, who first founded cities and reared temples to the immortal gods, and first ruled Over men. This land the neighbours who dwell around call Haemonia. And in it stands Iolcus, my city, and in it many others, where they have not so much as heard the name of the Aeaean isle; yet there is a story that Minyas starting thence, Minyas son of Aeolus, built long ago the city of Orchomenus that borders on the Cadmeians. But why do I tell thee all this vain talk, of our home and of Minos' daughter, far-famed Ariadne, by which glorious name they called that lovely maiden of whom thou askest me? Would that, as Minos then was well inclined to Theseus for her sake, so may thy father be joined to us in friendship!"

Thus he spake, soothing her with gentle converse. But pangs most bitter stirred her heart and in grief did she address him with vehement words:

"In Hellas, I ween, this is fair—to pay heed to covenants; but Aeetes is not such a man among men as thou sayest was Pasiphae's husband, Minos; nor can I liken myself to Ariadne; wherefore speak not of guest-love. But only do thou, when thou hast reached Iolcus, remember me, and thee even in my parents' despite, will I remember. And from far off may a rumour come to me or some messenger-bird, when thou forgettest me; or me, even me, may swift blasts catch up and bear over the sea hence to Iolcus, that so I may cast reproaches in thy face and remind thee that it was by my good will thou didst escape. May I then be seated in thy halls, an unexpected guest!"

Thus she spake with piteous tears falling down her cheeks, and to her Jason replied: "Let the empty blasts wander at will, lady, and the messenger-bird, for vain is thy talk. But if thou comest to those abodes and to the land of Hellas, honoured and reverenced shalt thou be by women and men; and they shall worship thee even as a goddess, for that by thy counsel their sons came home again, their brothers and kinsmen, and stalwart husbands were saved from calamity. And in our bridal chamber shalt thou prepare our couch; and nothing shall come between our love till the doom of death fold us round."

Thus he spake; and her soul melted within her to hear his words; nevertheless she shuddered to behold the deeds of destruction to come. Poor wretch! Not long was she destined to refuse a home in Hellas. For thus Hera devised it, that Aeaean Medea might come to Iolcus for a bane to Pelias, forsaking her native land.

And now her handmaids, glancing at them from a distance, were grieving in silence; and the time of day required that the maiden should return home to her mother's side. But she thought not yet of departing, for her soul delighted both in his beauty and in his winsome words, but Aeson's son took heed, and spake at last, though late: "It is time to depart, lest the sunlight sink before we know it, and some stranger notice all; but again will we come and meet here."

So did they two make trial of one another thus far with gentle words; and thereafter parted. Jason hastened to return in joyous mood to his comrades and the ship, she to her handmaids; and they all together came near to meet her, but she marked them not at all as they thronged around. For her soul had soared aloft amid the clouds. And her feet of their own accord mounted the swift chariot, and with one hand she took the reins, and with the other the whip of cunning workmanship, to drive the mules; and they rushed hasting to the city and the palace. And when she was come Chalciope in grief for her sons questioned her; but Medea, distraught by swiftly-changing thoughts, neither heard her words nor was eager to speak in answer to her questions. But she sat upon a low stool at the foot of her couch, bending down, her cheek leaning on her left hand, and her eyes were wet with tears as she pondered what an evil deed she had taken part in by her counsels.

Now when Aeson's son had joined his comrades again in the spot where he had left them when he departed, he set out to go with them, telling them all the story, to the gathering of the heroes; and together they approached the ship. And when they saw Jason they embraced him and questioned him. And he told to all the counsels of the maiden and showed the dread charm; but Idas alone of his comrades sat apart biting down his wrath; and the rest joyous in heart, at the hour when the darkness of night stayed them, peacefully took thought for themselves. But at daybreak they sent two men to go to Aeetes and ask for the seed, first Telamon himself, dear to Ares, and with him Aethalides, Hermes' famous son. So they went and made no vain journey; but when they came, lordly Aeetes gave them for the contest the fell teeth of the Aonian dragon which Cadmus found in Ogygian Thebes when he came seeking for Europa and there slew—the warder of the spring of Ares. There he settled by the guidance of the heifer whom Apollo by his prophetic word granted him to lead him on his way. But the teeth the Tritonian goddess tore away from the dragon's jaws and bestowed as a gift upon Aeetes and the slayer. And Agenor's son, Cadmus, sowed them on the Aonian plains and founded an earthborn people of all who were left from the spear when Ares did the reaping; and the teeth Aeetes then readily gave to be borne to the ship, for he deemed not that Jason would bring the contest to an end, even though he should cast the yoke upon the oxen.

Far away in the west the sun was sailing beneath the dark earth, beyond the furthest hills of the Aethiopians; and Night was laying the yoke upon her steeds; and the heroes were preparing their beds by the hawsers. But Jason, as soon as the stars of Helice, the bright-gleaming bear, had set, and the air had all grown still under heaven, went to a desert spot, like some stealthy thief, with all that was needful; for beforehand in the daytime had he taken thought for everything; and Argus came bringing a ewe and milk from the flock; and them he took from the ship. But when the hero saw a place which was far away from the tread of men, in a clear meadow beneath the open sky, there first of all he bathed his tender body reverently in the sacred river; and round him he placed a dark robe, which Hypsipyle of Lemnos had given him aforetime, a memorial of many a loving embrace. Then he dug a pit in the ground of a cubit's depth and heaped up billets of wood, and over it he cut the throat of the sheep, and duly placed the carcase above; and he kindled the logs placing fire beneath, and poured over them mingled libations, calling on Hecate Brimo to aid him in the contests. And when he had called on her he drew back; and she heard him, the dread goddess, from the uttermost depths and came to the sacrifice of Aeson's son; and round her horrible serpents twined themselves among the oak boughs; and there was a gleam of countless torches; and sharply howled around her the hounds of hell. All the meadows trembled at her step; and the nymphs that haunt the marsh and the river shrieked, all who dance round that mead of Amarantian Phasis. And fear seized Aeson's son, but not even so did he turn round as his feet bore him forth, till he came back to his comrades; and now early dawn arose and shed her light above snowy Caucasus.

Then Aeetes arrayed his breast in the stiff corslet which Ares gave him when he had slain Phlegraean Mimas with his own hands; and upon his head he placed a golden helmet with four plumes, gleaming like the sun's round light when he first rises from Ocean. And he wielded his shield of many hides, and his spear, terrible, resistless; none of the heroes could have withstood its shock now that they had left behind Heracles far away, who alone could have met it in battle. For the king his well-fashioned chariot of swift steeds was held near at hand by Phaethon, for him to mount; and he mounted, and held the reins in his hands. Then from the city he drove along the broad highway, that he might be present at the contest; and with him countless multitude rushed forth. And as Poseidon rides, mounted in his chariot, to the

Isthmian contest or to Taenarus, or to Lerna's water, or through the grove of Hyantian Onchestus, and thereafter passes even to Calaureia with his steeds, and the Haemonian rock or well-wooded Geraestus; even so was Aeetes, lord of the Colchians, to behold.

Meanwhile, prompted by Medea, Jason steeped the charm in water and sprinkled with it his shield and sturdy spear, and sword; and his comrades round him made proof of his weapons with might and main, but could not bend that spear even a little, but it remained firm in their stalwart hands unbroken as before. But in furious rage with them Idas, Aphareus' son, with his great sword hewed at the spear near the butt, and the edge leapt back repelled by the shock, like a hammer from the anvil; and the heroes shouted with joy for their hope in the contest. And then he sprinkled his body, and terrible prowess entered into him, unspeakable, dauntless; and his hands on both sides thrilled vigorously as they swelled with strength. And as when a warlike steed eager for the fight neighs and beats the ground with his hoof, while rejoicing he lifts his neck on high with ears erect; in such wise did Aeson's son rejoice in the strength of his limbs. And often hither and thither did he leap high in air tossing in his hands his shield of bronze and ashen spear. Thou wouldst say that wintry lightning flashing from the gloomy sky kept on darting forth from the clouds what time they bring with them their blackest rainstorm. Not long after that were the heroes to hold back from the contests; but sitting in rows on their benches they sped swiftly on to the plain of Ares. And it lay in front of them on the opposite side of the city, as far off as is the turning-post that a chariot must reach from the starting-point, when the kinsmen of a dead king appoint funeral games for footmen and horsemen. And they found Aeetes and the tribes of the Colchians; these were stationed on the Caucasian heights, but the king by the winding brink of the river.

Now Aeson's son, as soon as his comrades had made the hawsers fast, leapt from the ship, and with spear and shield came forth to the contest; and at the same time he took the gleaming helmet of bronze filled with sharp teeth, and his sword girt round his shoulders, his body stripped, in somewise resembling Ares and in somewise Apollo of the golden sword. And gazing over the field he saw the bulls' yoke of bronze and near it the plough, all of one piece, of stubborn adamant. Then he came near, and fixed his sturdy spear upright on its butt, and taking his helmet off leant it against the spear. And he went forward with shield alone to examine the countless tracks of the bulls, and they from some unseen lair beneath the earth, where was their strong steading, wrapt in murky smoke, both rushed out together, breathing forth flaming fire. And sore afraid were the heroes at the sight. But Jason, setting wide his feet, withstood their onset, as in the sea a rocky reef withstands the waves tossed by the countless blasts. Then in front of him he held his shield; and both the bulls with loud bellowing attacked him with their mighty horns; nor did they stir him a jot by their onset. And as when through the holes of the furnace the armourers' bellows anon gleam brightly, kindling the ravening flame, and anon cease from blowing, and a terrible roar rises from the fire when it darts up from below; so the bulls roared, breathing forth swift flame from their mouths, while the consuming heat played round him, smiting like lightning; but the maiden's charms protected him. Then grasping the tip of the horn of the right-hand bull, he dragged it mightily with all his strength to bring it near the yoke of bronze, and forced it down on to its knees, suddenly striking with his foot the foot of bronze. So also he threw the other bull on to its knees as it rushed upon him, and smote it down with one blow. And throwing to the ground his broad shield, he held them both down where they had fallen on their fore-knees, as he strode from side to side, now here, now there, and rushed swiftly through the flame. But Aeetes marvelled at the hero's might. And meantime the sons of Tyndareus— for long since had it been thus ordained for them—near at hand gave him the yoke from the ground to cast round them. Then tightly did he bind their necks; and lifting the pole of bronze between them, he fastened it to the yoke by its golden tip. So the twin heroes started back from the fire to the ship. But Jason took up again his shield and cast it on his back behind him, and grasped the strong helmet filled with sharp teeth, and his resistless spear, wherewith, like some ploughman with a Pelasgian goad, he pricked the bulls beneath, striking their flanks; and very firmly did he guide the well fitted plough handle, fashioned of adamant.

The bulls meantime raged exceedingly, breathing forth furious flame of fire; and their breath rose up like the roar of blustering winds, in fear of which above all seafaring men furl their large sail. But not long after that they moved on at the bidding of the spear; and behind them the rugged fallow was broken up, cloven by the might of the bulls and the sturdy ploughman. Then terribly groaned the clods withal along the furrows of the plough as they were rent, each a man's burden; and Jason followed, pressing down the cornfield with firm foot; and far from him

APOLLONIUS OF RHODES

he ever sowed the teeth along the clods as each was ploughed, turning his head back for fear lest the deadly crop of earthborn men should rise against him first; and the bulls toiled onwards treading with their hoofs of bronze.

But when the third part of the day was still left as it wanes from dawn, and wearied labourers call for the sweet hour of unyoking to come to them straightway, then the fallow was ploughed by the tireless ploughman, four plough-gates though it was; and he loosed the plough from the oxen. Them he scared in flight towards the plain; but he went back again to the ship, while he still saw the furrows free of the earthborn men. And all round his comrades heartened him with their shouts. And in the helmet he drew from the river's stream and quenched his thirst with the water. Then he bent his knees till they grew supple, and filled his mighty heart with courage, raging like a boar, when it sharpens its teeth against the hunters, while from its wrathful mouth plenteous foam drips to the ground. By now the earthborn men were springing up over all the field; and the plot of Ares, the death-dealer, bristled with sturdy shields and double-pointed spears and shining helmets; and the gleam reached Olympus from beneath, flashing through the air. And as when abundant snow has fallen on the earth and the storm blasts have dispersed the wintry clouds under the murky night, and all the hosts of the stars appear shining through the gloom; so did those warriors shine springing up above the earth. But Jason bethought him of the counsels of Medea full of craft, and seized from the plain a huge round boulder, a terrible quoit of Ares Enyalius; four stalwart youths could not have raised it from the ground even a little. Taking it in his hands he threw it with a rush far away into their midst; and himself crouched unseen behind his shield, with full confidence. And the Colchians gave a loud cry, like the roar of the sea when it beats upon sharp crags; and speechless amazement seized Aeetes at the rush of the sturdy quoit. And the Earthborn, like fleet-footed hounds, leaped upon one another and slew with loud yells; and on earth their mother they fell beneath their own spears, likes pines or oaks, which storms of wind beat down. And even as a fiery star leaps from heaven, trailing a furrow of light, a portent to men, whoever see it darting with a gleam through the dusky sky; in such wise did Aeson's son rush upon the earthborn men, and he drew from the sheath his bare sword, and smote here and there, mowing them down, many on the belly and side, half risen to the air—and some that had risen as far as the shoulders—and some just standing upright, and others even now rushing to battle. And as when a fight is stirred up concerning boundaries, and a husbandman, in fear lest they should ravage his fields, seizes in his hand a curved sickle, newly sharpened, and hastily cuts the unripe crop, and waits not for it to be parched in due season by the beams of the sun; so at that time did Jason cut down the crop of the Earthborn; and the furrows were filled with blood, as the channels of a spring with water. And they fell, some on their faces biting the rough clod of earth with their teeth, some on their backs, and others on their hands and sides, like to sea-monsters to behold. And many, smitten before raising their feet from the earth, bowed down as far to the ground as they had risen to the air, and rested there with the damp of death on their brows. Even so, I ween, when Zeus has sent a measureless rain, new planted orchard-shoots droop to the ground, cut off by the root—the toil of gardening men; but heaviness of heart and deadly anguish come to the owner of the farm, who planted them; so at that time did bitter grief come upon the heart of King Aeetes. And he went back to the city among the Colchians, pondering how he might most quickly oppose the heroes. And the day died, and Jason's contest was ended.

Book IV

Now do thou thyself, goddess Muse, daughter of Zeus, tell of the labour and wiles of the Colchian maiden. Surely my soul within me wavers with speechless amazement as I ponder whether I should call it the lovesick grief of mad passion or a panic flight, through which she left the Colchian folk.

Aeetes all night long with the bravest captains of his people was devising in his halls sheer treachery against the heroes, with fierce wrath in his heart at the issue of the hateful contest; nor did he deem at all that these things were being accomplished without the knowledge of his daughters.

But into Medea's heart Hera cast most grievous fear; and she trembled like a nimble fawn whom the baying of hounds hath terrified amid the thicket of a deep copse. For at once she truly foreboded that the aid she had given was not hidden from her father, and that quickly she would fill up the cup of woe. And she dreaded the guilty knowledge of her handmaids; her eyes were filled with fire and her ears rung with a terrible cry. Often did she clutch at her throat, and often did she drag out her hair by the roots and groan in wretched despair. There on that very day the maiden would have tasted the drugs and perished and so have made void the purposes of Hera, had not the goddess driven her, all bewildered, to flee with the sons of Phrixus; and her fluttering soul within her was comforted; and then she poured from her bosom all the drugs back again into the casket. Then she kissed her bed, and the folding-doors on both sides, and stroked the walls, and tearing away in her hands a long tress of hair, she left it in the chamber for her mother, a memorial of her maidenhood, and thus lamented with passionate voice:

"I go, leaving this long tress here in my stead, O mother mine; take this farewell from me as I go far hence; farewell Chalciope, and all my home. Would that the sea, stranger, had dashed thee to pieces, ere thou earnest to the Colchian land!"

Thus she spake, and from her eyes shed copious tears. And as a bondmaid steals away from a wealthy house, whom fate has lately severed from her native land, nor yet has she made trial of grievous toil, but still unschooled to misery and shrinking in terror from slavish tasks, goes about beneath the cruel hands of a mistress; even so the lovely maiden rushed forth from her home. But to her the bolts of the doors gave way self-moved, leaping backwards at the swift strains of her magic song. And with bare feet she sped along the narrow paths, with her left hand holding her robe over her brow to veil her face and fair cheeks, and with her right lifting up the hem of her tunic. Quickly along the dark track, outside the towers of the spacious city, did she come in fear; nor did any of the warders note her, but she sped on unseen by them. Thence she was minded to go to the temple; for well she knew the way, having often aforetime wandered there in quest of corpses and noxious roots of the earth, as a sorceress is wont to do; and her soul fluttered with quivering fear. And the Titanian goddess, the moon, rising from a far land, beheld her as she fled distraught, and fiercely exulted over her, and thus spake to her own heart:

"Not I alone then stray to the Latmian cave, nor do I alone burn with love for fair Endymion; oft times with thoughts of love have I been driven away by thy crafty spells, in order that in the darkness of night thou mightest work thy sorcery at ease, even the deeds dear to thee. And now thou thyself too hast part in a like mad passion; and some god of affliction has given thee Jason to be thy grievous woe. Well, go on, and steel thy heart, wise though thou be, to take up thy burden of pain, fraught with many sighs."

"Thus spake the goddess; but swiftly the maiden's feet bore her, hasting on. And gladly did she gain the high bank of the river and beheld on the opposite side the gleam of fire, which all night long the heroes were kindling in joy at the contest's issue. Then through the gloom, with clear-pealing voice from across the stream, she called on Phrontis, the youngest of Phrixus' sons, and he with his brothers and Aeson's son recognised the maiden's *voice*; and in silence his comrades wondered when they knew that it was so in truth. Thrice she called, and thrice at the bidding of the company Phrontis called out in reply; and meantime the heroes were rowing with swift-moving oars in search of her. Not yet were they casting the ship's hawsers upon the opposite bank, when Jason with light feet leapt to land from the deck above, and after him Phrontis and Argus, sons of Phrixus, leapt to the ground; and she, clasping their knees with both hands, thus addressed them:

"Save me, the hapless one, my friends, from Aeetes, and yourselves too, for all is brought to light, nor doth any remedy come. But let us flee upon the ship; before the king mounts his swift chariot. And I will lull to sleep the guardian serpent and give you the fleece of gold; but do thou, stranger, amid thy comrades make the gods witness of the vows thou hast taken on thyself for my sake; and now that I have fled far from my country, make me not a mark for blame and dishonour for want of kinsmen."

She spake in anguish; but greatly did the heart of Aeson's son rejoice, and at once, as she fell at his knees, he raised her gently and embraced her, and spake words of comfort: "Lady, let Zeus of Olympus himself be witness to my oath, and Hera, queen of marriage, bride of Zeus, that I will set thee in my halls my own wedded wife, when we have reached the land of Hellas on our return."

Thus he spake, and straightway clasped her right hand in his; and she bade them row the swift ship to the sacred grove near at hand, in order that, while it was still night, they might seize and carry off the fleece against the will of Aeetes. Word and deed were one to the eager crew. For they took her on board, and straightway thrust the ship from shore; and loud was the din as the chieftains strained at their oars, but she, starting back, held out her hands in despair towards the shore. But Jason spoke cheering words and restrained her grief.

Now at the hour when men have cast sleep from their eyes—huntsmen, who, trusting to their hounds, never slumber away the end of night, but avoid the light of dawn lest, smiting with its white beams, it efface the track and scent of the quarry—then did Aeson's son and the maiden step forth from the ship over a grassy spot, the "Ram's couch" as men call it, where it first bent its wearied knees in rest, bearing on its back the Minyan son of Athamas. And close by, all smirched with soot, was the base of the altar, which the Aeolid Phrixus once set up to Zeus, the aider of fugitives, when he sacrificed the golden wonder at the bidding of Hermes who graciously met him on the way. There by the counsels of Argus the chieftains put them ashore.

And they two by the pathway came to the sacred grove, seeking the huge oak tree on which was hung the fleece, like to a cloud that blushes red with the fiery beams of the rising sun. But right in front the serpent with his keen sleepless eyes saw them coming, and stretched out his long neck and hissed in awful wise; and all round the long banks of the river echoed and the boundless grove. Those heard it who dwelt in the Colchian land very far from Titanian Aea, near the outfall of Lycus, the river which parts from loud-roaring Araxes and blends his sacred stream with Phasis, and they twain flow on together in one and pour their waters into the Caucasian Sea. And through fear young mothers awoke, and round their new-born babes, who were sleeping in their arms, threw their hands in agony, for the small limbs started at that hiss. And as when above a pile of smouldering wood countless eddies of smoke roll up mingled with soot, and one ever springs up quickly after another, rising aloft from beneath in wavering wreaths; so at that time did that monster roll his countless coils covered with hard dry scales. And as he writhed, the maiden came before his eyes, with sweet voice calling to her aid Sleep, highest of gods, to charm the monster; and she cried to the queen of the underworld, the night-wanderer, to be propitious to her enterprise. And Aeson's son followed in fear, but the serpent, already charmed by her song, was relaxing the long ridge of his giant spine, and lengthening out his myriad coils, like a dark wave, dumb and noiseless, rolling over a sluggish sea; but still he raised aloft his grisly head, eager to enclose them both in his murderous jaws. But she with a newly cut spray of juniper, dipping and drawing untempered charms from her mystic brew, sprinkled his eyes, while she chanted her song; and all around the potent scent of the charm cast sleep; and on the very spot he let his jaw sink down; and far behind through the wood with its many trees were those countless coils stretched out.

Hereupon Jason snatched the golden fleece from the oak, at the maiden's bidding; and she, standing firm, smeared with the charm the monster's head, till Jason himself bade her turn back towards their ship, and she left the grove of Ares, dusky with shade. And as a maiden catches on her finely wrought robe the gleam of the moon at the full, as it rises above her high-roofed chamber; and her heart rejoices as she beholds the fair ray; so at that time did Jason uplift the mighty fleece in his hands; and from the shimmering of the flocks of wool there settled on his fair cheeks and brow a red flush like a flame. And great as is the hide of a yearling ox or stag, which huntsmen call a brocket, so great in extent was the fleece all golden above. Heavy it was, thickly clustered with flocks; and as he moved along, even beneath his feet the sheen rose up from the earth. And he strode on now with the fleece covering his left shoulder from the height of his neck to his feet, and now again he gathered it up in his hands; for he feared exceedingly, lest some god or man should meet him and deprive him thereof.

Dawn was spreading over the earth when they reached the throng of heroes; and the youths marvelled to behold the mighty fleece, which gleamed like the lightning of Zeus. And each one started up eager to touch it and clasp it in his hands. But the son of Aeson restrained them all, and threw over it a mantle newly-woven; and he led the maiden to the stern and seated her there, and spake to them all as follows:

"No longer now, my friends, forbear to return to your fatherland. For now the task for which we dared this grievous voyage, toiling with bitter sorrow of heart, has been lightly fulfilled by the maiden's counsels. Her—for such is her will—I will bring home to be my wedded wife; do ye preserve her, the glorious saviour of all Achaea and of yourselves. For of a surety, I ween, will Aeetes come with his host to bar our passage from the river into the sea. But do some of you toil at the oars in turn, sitting man by man; and half of you raise your shields of oxhide, a ready defence against the darts of the enemy, and guard our return. And now in our hands we hold the fate of our children and dear country and of our aged parents; and on our venture all Hellas depends, to reap either the shame of failure or great renown."

Thus he spake, and donned his armour of war; and they cried aloud, wondrously eager. And he drew his sword from the sheath and cut the hawsers at the stern. And near the maiden he took his stand ready armed by the steersman Ancaeus, and with their rowing the ship sped on as they strained desperately to drive her clear of the river.

By this time Medea's love and deeds had become known to haughty Aeetes and to all the Colchians. And they thronged to the assembly in arms; and countless as the waves of the stormy sea when they rise crested by the wind, or as the leaves that fall to the ground from the wood with its myriad branches in the month when the leaves fall—who could reckon their tale?—so they in countless number poured along the banks of the river shouting in frenzy; and in his shapely chariot Aeetes shone forth above all with his steeds, the gift of Helios, swift as the blasts of the wind. In his left hand he raised his curved shield, and in his right a huge pine-torch, and near him in front stood up his mighty spear. And Apsyrtus held in his hands the reins of the steeds. But already the ship was cleaving the sea before her, urged on by stalwart oarsmen, and the stream of the mighty river rushing down. But the king in grievous anguish lifted his hands and called on Helios and Zeus to bear witness to their evil deeds; and terrible threats he uttered against all his people, that unless they should with their own hands seize the maiden, either on the land or still finding the ship on the swell of the open sea, and bring her back, that so he might satisfy his eager soul with vengeance for all those deeds, at the cost of their own lives they should learn and abide all his rage and revenge.

Thus spake Aeetes; and on that same day the Colchians launched their ships and cast the tackle on board, and on that same day sailed forth on the sea; thou wouldst not say so mighty a host was a fleet of ships, but that a countless flight of birds, swarm on swarm, was clamouring over the sea.

Swiftly the wind blew, as the goddess Hera planned, so that most quickly Aeaean Medea might reach the Pelasgian land, a bane to the house of Pelias, and on the third morn they bound the ship's stern cables to the shores of the Paphlagonians, at the mouth of the river Halys. For Medea bade them land and propitiate Hecate with sacrifice. Now all that the maiden prepared for offering the sacrifice may no man know, and may my soul not urge me to sing thereof. Awe restrains my lips, yet from that time the altar which the heroes raised on the beach to the goddess remains till now, a sight to men of a later day.

And straightway Aeson's son and the rest of the heroes bethought them of Phineus, how that he had said that their course from Aea should be different, but to all alike his meaning was dim. Then Argus spake, and they eagerly hearkened:

"We go to Orchomenus, whither that unerring seer, whom ye met aforetime, foretold your voyage. For there is another course, signified by those priests of the immortal gods, who have sprung from Tritonian Thebes. As yet all the stars that wheel in the heaven were not, nor yet, though one should inquire, could aught be heard of the sacred race of the Danai. Apidanean Arcadians alone existed, Arcadians who lived even before the moon, it is said, eating acorns on the hills; nor at that time was the Pelasgian land ruled by the glorious sons of Deucalion, in the days when Egypt, mother of men of an older time, was called the fertile Morning-land, and the river fair-flowing Triton, by which all the Morning-land is watered; and never does the rain from Zeus moisten the earth; but from the flooding of the river abundant crops spring up. From this land, it is said, a king[27] made his way all round through the whole of Europe and Asia, trusting in the might and strength and courage of his people; and countless cities did he found wherever he came, whereof some are still inhabited and some not; many an age hath passed since then. But Aea abides unshaken even now and the sons of those men whom that king settled to dwell in Aea. They preserve the writings of their fathers, graven on pillars, whereon are marked all the ways and the limits of sea and land as ye journey on all sides round. There is a river, the uttermost horn of Ocean, broad and exceeding deep,

---

27. The allusion is to Sesostris, see Herod, ii. 102 foll.

APOLLONIUS OF RHODES

that a merchant ship may traverse; they call it Ister and have marked it far off; and for a while it cleaves the boundless tilth alone in one stream; for beyond the blasts of the north wind, far off in the Rhipaean mountains, its springs burst forth with a roar. But when it enters the boundaries of the Thracians and Scythians, here, dividing its stream into two, it sends its waters partly into the Ionian sea,[28] and partly to the south into a deep gulf that bends upwards from the Trinacrian sea, that sea which lies along your land, if indeed Achelous flows forth from your land."

Thus he spake, and to them the goddess granted a happy portent, and all at the sight shouted approval, that this was their appointed path. For before them appeared a trail of heavenly light, a sign where they might pass. And gladly they left behind there the son of Lycus and with canvas outspread sailed over the sea, with their eyes on the Paphlagonian mountains. But they did not round Carambis, for the winds and the gleam of the heavenly fire stayed with them till they reached Ister's mighty stream.

Now some of the Colchians, in a vain search, passed out from Pontus through the Cyanean rocks; but the rest went to the river, and them Apsyrtus led, and, turning aside, he entered the mouth called Fair. Wherefore he outstripped the heroes by crossing a neck of land into the furthest gulf of the Ionian sea. For a certain island is enclosed by Ister, by name Peuce, three-cornered, its base stretching along the coast, and with a sharp angle towards the river; and round it the outfall is cleft in two. One mouth they call the mouth of Narex, and the other, at the lower end, the Fair mouth. And through this Apsyrtus and his Colchians rushed with all speed; but the heroes went upwards far away towards the highest part of the island. And in the meadows the country shepherds left their countless flocks for dread of the ships, for they deemed that they were beasts coming forth from the monster-teeming sea. For never yet before had they seen seafaring ships, neither the Scythians mingled with the Thracians, nor the Sigynni, nor yet the Graucenii, nor the Sindi that now inhabit the vast desert plain of Laurium. But when they had passed near the mount Angurum, and the cliff of Cauliacus, far from the mount Angurum, round which Ister, dividing his stream, falls into the sea on this side

---

28. Or, reading, "into our sea." The Euxine is meant in any case and the word Ionian is therefore wrong.

and on that, and the Laurian plain, then indeed the Colchians went forth into the Cronian sea and cut off all the ways, to prevent their foes' escape. And the heroes came down the river behind and reached the two Brygean isles of Artemis near at hand. Now in one of them was a sacred temple; and on the other they landed, avoiding the host of Apsyrtus; for the Colchians had left these islands out of many within the river, just as they were, through reverence for the daughter of Zeus; but the rest, thronged by the Colchians, barred the ways to the sea. And so on other islands too, close by, Apsyrtus left his host as far as the river Salangon and the Nestian land.

There the Minyae would at that time have yielded in grim fight, a few to many; but ere then they made a covenant, shunning a dire quarrel; as to the golden fleece, that since Aeetes himself had so promised them if they should fulfil the contests, they should keep it as justly won, whether they carried it off by craft or even openly in the king's despite; but as to Medea—for that was the cause of strife—that they should give her in ward to Leto's daughter apart from the throng, until some one of the kings that dispense justice should utter his doom, whether she must return to her father's home or follow the chieftains to the land of Hellas.

Now when the maiden had mused upon all this, sharp anguish shook her heart unceasingly; and quickly she called forth Jason alone apart from his comrades, and led him aside until they were far away, and before his face uttered her speech all broken with sobs:

"What is this purpose that ye are now devising about me, O son of Aeson? Has thy triumph utterly cast forgetfulness upon thee, and reckest thou nothing of all that thou spakest when held fast by necessity? whither are fled the oaths by Zeus the suppliants' god, whither are fled thy honied promises? for which in no seemly wise, with shameless will, I have left my country, the glories of my home and even my parents— things that were dearest to me; and far away all alone I am borne over the sea with the plaintive kingfishers because of thy trouble, in order that I might save thy life in fulfilling the contests with the oxen and the earthborn men. Last of all the fleece—when the matter became known, it was by my folly thou didst win it; and a foul reproach have I poured on womankind. Wherefore I say that as thy child, thy bride and thy sister, I follow thee to the land of Hellas. Be ready to stand by me to the end, abandon me not left forlorn of thee when thou dost visit the kings. But only save me; let justice and right, to which we have both agreed, stand firm; or else do thou at once shear through this neck with the sword, that I may gain the guerdon due to my mad passion. Poor wretch! if the king, to whom you both commit your cruel covenant, doom me to belong to my brother. How shall I come to my father's sight? Will it be with a good name? What revenge, what heavy calamity shall I not endure in agony for the terrible deeds I have done? And wilt thou win the return that thy heart desires? Never may Zeus' bride, the queen of all, in whom thou dost glory, bring that to pass. Mayst thou some time remember me when thou art racked with anguish; may the fleece like a dream vanish into the nether darkness on the wings of the wind! And may my avenging Furies forthwith drive thee from thy country, for all that I have suffered through thy cruelty! These curses will not be allowed to fall unaccomplished to the ground. A mighty oath hast thou transgressed, ruthless one; but not long shalt thou and thy comrades sit at ease casting eyes of mockery upon me, for all your covenants."

Thus she spake, seething with fierce wrath; and she longed to set fire to the ship and to hew it utterly in pieces, and herself to fall into the raging flame. But Jason, half afraid, thus addressed her with gentle words:

"Forbear, lady; me too this pleases not. But we seek some respite from battle, for such a cloud of hostile men, like to a fire, surrounds us, on thy account. For all that inhabit this land are eager to aid Apsyrtus, that they may lead thee back home to thy father, like some captured maid. And all of us would perish in hateful destruction, if we closed with them in fight; and bitterer still will be the pain, if we are slain and leave thee to be their prey. But this covenant will weave a web of guile to lead him to ruin. Nor will the people of the land for thy sake oppose us, to favour the Colchians, when their prince is no longer with them, who is thy champion and thy brother; nor will I shrink from matching myself in fight with the Colchians, if they bar my way homeward."

Thus he spake soothing her; and she uttered a deadly speech: "Take heed now. For when sorry deeds are done we must needs devise sorry counsel, since at first I was distraught by my error, and by heaven's will it was I wrought the accomplishment of evil desires. Do thou in the turmoil shield me from the Colchians' spears; and I will beguile Apsyrtus to come into thy hands—do thou greet him with splendid gifts—if only I could persuade the heralds on their departure to bring him alone to hearken to my words. Thereupon if this deed pleases thee, slay him and raise a conflict with the Colchians, I care not."

So they two agreed and prepared a great web of guile for Apsyrtus, and provided many gifts such as are due to guests, and among them gave a sacred robe of Hypsipyle, of crimson hue. The Graces with their own hands had wrought it for Dionysus in sea-girt Dia, and he gave it to his son Thoas thereafter, and Thoas left it to Hypsipyle, and she gave that fair-wrought guest-gift with many another marvel to Aeson's son to wear. Never couldst thou satisfy thy sweet desire by touching it or gazing on it. And from it a divine fragrance breathed from the time when the king of Nysa himself lay to rest thereon, flushed with wine and nectar as he clasped the beauteous breast of the maiden-daughter of Minos, whom once Theseus forsook in the island of Dia, when she had followed him from Cnossus. And when she had worked upon the heralds to induce her brother to come, as soon as she reached the temple of the goddess, according to the agreement, and the darkness of night surrounded them that so she might devise with him a cunning plan for her to take the mighty fleece of gold and return to the home of Aeetes, for, she said, the sons of Phrixus had given her by force to the strangers to carry off; with such beguiling words she scattered to the air and the breezes her witching charms, which even from afar would have drawn down the savage beast from the steep mountain-height.

Ruthless Love, great bane, great curse to mankind, from thee come deadly strifes and lamentations and groans, and countless pains as well have their stormy birth from thee. Arise, thou god, and arm thyself against the sons of our foes in such guise as when thou didst fill Medea's heart with accursed madness. How then by evil doom did she slay Apsyrtus when he came to meet her? For that must our song tell next.

When the heroes had left the maiden on the island of Artemis, according to the covenant, both sides ran their ships to land separately. And Jason went to the ambush to lie in wait for Apsyrtus and then for his comrades. But he, beguiled by these dire promises, swiftly crossed the swell of the sea in his ship, and in dark night set foot on the sacred island; and faring all alone to meet her he made trial in speech of his sister, as a tender child tries a wintry torrent which not even strong men can pass through, to see if she would devise some guile against the strangers. And so they two agreed together on everything; and straightway Aeson's son leapt forth from the thick ambush, lifting his bare sword in his hand, and quickly the maiden turned her eyes aside and covered them with her veil that she might not see the blood of her brother when he was smitten. And Jason marked him and struck him down, as a butcher strikes down a mighty strong-horned bull, hard by the temple which the Brygi on the mainland opposite had once built for Artemis. In its vestibule he fell on his knees; and at last the hero breathing out his life caught up in both hands the dark blood as it welled from the wound; and he dyed with red his sister's silvery veil and robe as she shrank away. And with swift side-glance the irresistible pitiless Fury beheld the deadly deed they had done. And the hero, Aeson's son, cut off the extremities of the dead man, and thrice licked up some blood and thrice spat the pollution from his teeth, as it is right for the slayer to do, to atone for a treacherous murder. And the clammy corpse he hid in the ground where even now those bones lie among the Apsyrtians.

Now as soon as the heroes saw the blaze of a torch, which the maiden raised for them as a sign to pursue, they laid their own ship near the Colchian ship, and they slaughtered the Colchian host, as kites slay the tribes of wood-pigeons, or as lions of the wold, when they have leapt amid the steading, drive a great flock of sheep huddled together. Nor did one of them escape death, but the heroes rushed upon the whole crew, destroying them like a flame; and at last Jason met them, and was eager to give aid where none was needed; but already they were taking thought for him too. Thereupon they sat to devise some prudent counsel for their voyage, and the maiden came upon them as they pondered, but Peleus spake his word first:

"I now bid you embark while it is still night, and take with your oars the passage opposite to that which the enemy guards, for at dawn when they see their plight I deem that no word urging to further pursuit of us will prevail with them; but as people bereft of their king, they will be scattered in grievous dissension. And easy, when the people are scattered, will this path be for us on our return."

Thus he spake; and the youths assented to the words of Aeacus' son. And quickly they entered the ship, and toiled at their oars unceasingly until they reached the sacred isle of Electra, the highest of them all, near the river Eridanus.

But when the Colchians learnt the death of their prince, verily they were eager to pursue *Argo* and the Minyans through all the Cronian sea. But Hera restrained them by terrible lightnings from the sky. And at last they loathed their own homes in the Cytaean land, quailing before Aeetes' fierce wrath; so they landed and made abiding homes there, scattered far and wide. Some set foot on those very islands where the heroes had stayed, and they still dwell there, bearing a name derived from Apsyrtus; and others built a fenced city by the dark deep Illyrian river, where is the tomb of Harmonia and Cadmus, dwelling among the Encheleans; and others live amid the mountains which are called the Thunderers, from the day when the thunders of Zeus, son of Cronos, prevented them from crossing over to the island opposite.

Now the heroes, when their return seemed safe for them, fared onward and made their hawsers fast to the land of the Hylleans. For the islands lay thick in the river and made the path dangerous for those who sailed thereby. Nor, as aforetime, did the Hylleans devise their hurt, but of their own accord furthered their passage, winning as guerdon a mighty tripod of Apollo. For tripods twain had Phoebus given to Aeson's son to carry afar in the voyage he had to make, at the time when he went to sacred Pytho to enquire about this very voyage; and it was ordained by fate that in whatever land they should be placed, that land should never be ravaged by the attacks of foemen. Therefore even now this tripod is hidden in that land near the pleasant city of Hyllus, far beneath the earth, that it may ever be unseen by mortals. Yet they found not King Hyllus still alive in the land, whom fair Melite bare to Heracles in the land of the Phaeacians. For he came to the abode of Nausithous and to Macris, the nurse of Dionysus, to cleanse himself from the deadly murder of his children; here he loved and overcame the water nymph Melite, the daughter of the river Aegaeus, and she bare mighty Hyllus. But when he had grown up he desired not to dwell in that island under the rule of Nausithous the king; but he collected a host of native Phaeacians and came to the Cronian sea; for the hero King Nausithous aided his journey, and there he settled, and the Mentores slew him as he was fighting for the oxen of his field.

Now, goddesses, say how it is that beyond this sea, near the land of Ausonia and the Ligystian isles, which are called Stoechades, the mighty tracks of the ship *Argo* are clearly sung of? What great constraint and need brought the heroes so far? What breezes wafted them?

When Apsyrtus had fallen in mighty overthrow Zeus himself, king of gods, was seized with wrath at what they had done. And he ordained that by the counsels of Aeaean Circe they should cleanse themselves from the terrible stain of blood and suffer countless woes before their return. Yet none of the chieftains knew this; but far onward they sped starting from the Hyllean land, and they left behind all the islands that were beforetime thronged by the Colchians—the Liburnian isles, isle after isle, Issa, Dysceladus, and lovely Pityeia. Next after them they came to Corcyra, where Poseidon settled the daughter of Asopus, fair-haired Corcyra, far from the land of Phlius, whence he had carried her off through love; and sailors beholding it from the sea, all black with its sombre woods, call it Corcyra the Black. And next they passed Melite, rejoicing in the soft-blowing breeze, and steep Cerossus, and Nymphaea at a distance, where lady Calypso, daughter of Atlas, dwelt; and they deemed they saw the misty mountains of Thunder. And then Hera bethought her of the counsels and wrath of Zeus concerning them. And she devised an ending of their voyage and stirred up storm-winds before them, by which they were caught and borne back to the rocky isle of Electra. And straightway on a sudden there called to them in the midst of their course, speaking with a human voice, the beam of the hollow ship, which Athena had set in the centre of the stem, made of Dodonian oak. And deadly fear seized them as they heard the voice that told of the grievous wrath of Zeus. For it proclaimed that they should not escape the paths of an endless sea nor grievous tempests, unless Circe should purge away the guilt of the ruthless murder of Apsyrtus; and it bade Polydeuces and Castor pray to the immortal gods first to grant a path through the Ausonian sea where they should find Circe, daughter of Perse and Helios.

Thus *Argo* cried through the darkness; and the sons of Tyndareus uprose, and lifted their hands to the immortals praying for each boon: but dejection held the rest of the Minyan heroes. And far on sped *Argo* under sail, and entered deep into the stream of Eridanus; where once, smitten on the breast by the blazing bolt, Phaëthon half-consumed fell from the chariot of Helios into the opening of that deep lake; and even now it belcheth up heavy steam clouds from the smouldering wound. And no bird spreading its light wings can cross that water; but in mid-course it plunges into the flame, fluttering. And all around the maidens, the daughters of Helios, enclosed in tall poplars, wretchedly wail a piteous plaint; and from their eyes they shed on the ground bright drops of amber. These are dried by the sun upon the sand; but whenever the waters of the dark lake flow over the strand before the blast of the wailing wind, then they roll on in a mass into Eridanus with swelling tide. But the Celts have attached this story to them, that these are the tears of Leto's son, Apollo, that are borne along by the eddies, the countless tears that he shed aforetime when he came to the sacred race of the Hyperboreans and left shining heaven at the chiding of his father, being in wrath concerning his son whom divine Coronis bare in bright Lacereia at the mouth of Amyrus. And such is the story told among these men. But no desire for food or drink seized the heroes nor were their thoughts turned to joy. But they were sorely afflicted all day, heavy and faint at heart, with the noisome stench, hard to endure, which the streams of Eridanus sent forth from Phaethon still burning; and at night they heard the piercing lament of the daughters of Helios, wailing with shrill voice; and, as they lamented, their tears were borne on the water like drops of oil.

Thence they entered the deep stream of Rhodanus which flows into Eridanus; and where they meet there is a roar of mingling waters. Now that river, rising from the ends of the earth, where are the portals and mansions of Night, on one side bursts forth upon the beach of Ocean, at another pours into the Ionian sea, and on the third through seven mouths sends its stream to the Sardinian sea and its limitless bay.[29] And from Rhodanus they entered stormy lakes, which spread throughout the Celtic mainland of wondrous size; and there they would have met with an inglorious calamity; for a certain branch of the river was bearing them towards a gulf of Ocean which in ignorance they were about to enter, and never would they have returned from there in safety. But Hera leaping forth from heaven pealed her cry from the Hercynian rock; and all together were shaken with fear of her cry; for terribly crashed the mighty firmament. And backward they turned by reason of the goddess, and noted the path by which their return was ordained. And after a long while they came to the beach of the surging sea by the devising of Hera, passing unharmed through countless tribes of the Celts and Ligyans. For round them the goddess poured a dread mist day by day as they fared on. And sailing through the midmost mouth, they reached the Stoechades islands in safety by the aid of the sons of Zeus; wherefore altars and sacred rites are established in their honour for ever; and not that sea-faring alone did they attend to succour; but Zeus granted to them the ships of future sailors too. Then leaving the Stoechades they passed on to the island Aethalia, where after their toil they wiped away with pebbles sweat in abundance; and pebbles like skin in colour are strewn on the beach[30]; and there are their quoits and their wondrous armour; and there is the Argoan harbour called after them.

---

29. Apollonius seems to have thought that the Po, the Rhone, and the Rhine are all connected together.

30. i.e. like the scrapings from skin,; see Strabo p. 224 for this adventure.

And quickly from there they passed through the sea, beholding the Tyrrhenian shores of Ausonia; and they came to the famous harbour of Aeaea, and from the ship they cast hawsers to the shore near at hand. And here they found Circe bathing her head in the salt sea-spray, for sorely had she been scared by visions of the night. With blood her chambers and all the walls of her palace seemed to be running, and flame was devouring all the magic herbs with which she used to bewitch strangers whoever came; and she herself with murderous blood quenched the glowing flame, drawing it up in her hands; and she ceased from deadly fear. Wherefore when morning came she rose, and with sea-spray was bathing her hair and her garments. And beasts, not resembling the beasts of the wild, nor yet like men in body, but with a medley of limbs, went in a throng, as sheep from the fold in multitudes follow the shepherd. Such creatures, compacted of various limbs, did earth herself produce from the primeval slime when she had not yet grown solid beneath a rainless sky nor yet had received a drop of moisture from the rays of the scorching sun; but time combined these forms and marshalled them in their ranks; in such wise these monsters shapeless of form followed her. And exceeding wonder seized the heroes, and at once, as each gazed on the form and face of Circe, they readily guessed that she was the sister of Aeetes.

Now when she had dismissed the fears of her nightly visions, straightway she fared backwards, and in her subtlety she bade the heroes follow, charming them on with her hand. Thereupon the host remained stedfast at the bidding of Aeson's son, but Jason drew with him the Colchian maid. And both followed the selfsame path till they reached the hall of Circe, and she in amaze at their coming bade them sit on brightly burnished seats. And they, quiet and silent, sped to the hearth and sat there, as is the wont of wretched suppliants. Medea hid her face in both her hands, but Jason fixed in the ground the mighty hilted sword with which he had slain Aeetes' son; nor did they raise their eyes to meet her look. And straightway Circe became aware of the doom of a suppliant and the guilt of murder. Wherefore in reverence for the ordinance of Zeus, the god of suppliants, who is a god of wrath yet mightily aids slayers of men, she began to offer the sacrifice with which ruthless suppliants are cleansed from guilt when they approach the altar. First to atone for the murder still unexpiated, she held above their heads the young of a sow whose dugs yet swelled from the fruit of the womb, and, severing its neck, sprinkled their hands with the blood; and again she made propitiation with other drink offerings, calling on Zeus the Cleanser, the protector of murder-stained suppliants. And all the defilements in a mass her attendants bore forth from the palace—the Naiad nymphs who ministered all things to her. And within, Circe, standing by the hearth, kept burning atonement-cakes without wine, praying the while that she might stay from their wrath the terrible Furies, and that Zeus himself might be propitious and gentle to them both, whether with hands stained by the blood of a stranger or, as kinsfolk, by the blood of a kinsman, they should implore his grace.

But when she had wrought all her task, then she raised them up and seated them on well polished seats, and herself sat near, face to face with them. And at once she asked them clearly of their business and their voyaging, and whence they had come to her land and palace, and had thus seated themselves as suppliants at her hearth. For in truth the hideous remembrance of her dreams entered her mind as she pondered; and she longed to hear the voice of the maiden, her kinswoman, as soon as she saw that she had raised her eyes from the ground. For all those of the race of Helios were plain to discern, since by the far flashing of their eyes they shot in front of them a gleam as of gold. So Medea told her all she asked—the daughter of Aeetes of the gloomy heart, speaking gently in the Colchian tongue, both of the quest and the journeyings of the heroes, and of their toils in the swift contests, and how she had sinned through the counsels of her much-sorrowing sister, and how with the sons of Phrixus she had fled afar from the tyrannous horrors of her father; but she shrank from telling of the murder of Apsyrtus. Yet she escaped not Circe's ken; nevertheless, in spite of all she pitied the weeping maiden, and spake thus:

"Poor wretch, an evil and shameful return hast thou planned. Not for long, I ween, wilt thou escape the heavy wrath of Aeetes; but soon will he go even to the dwellings of Hellas to avenge the blood of his son, for intolerable are the deeds thou hast done. But since thou art my suppliant and my kinswoman, no further ill shall I devise against thee at thy coming; but begone from my halls, companioning the stranger, whosoever he be, this unknown one that thou hast taken in thy father's despite; and kneel not to me at my hearth, for never will I approve thy counsels and thy shameful flight."

Thus she spake, and measureless anguish seized the maid; and over her eyes she cast her robe and poured forth a lamentation, until the hero took her by the hand and led her forth from the hall quivering with fear. So they left the home of Circe.

But they were not unmarked by the spouse of Zeus, son of Cronos; but Iris told her when she saw them faring from the hall. For Hera had bidden her watch what time they should come to the ship; so again she urged her and spake:

"Dear Iris, now come, if ever thou hast fulfilled bidding, his thee away on light pinions, and bid Thetis arise from the sea and come hither. For need of her is come upon me. Then go to the sea-beaches where the bronze anvils of Hephaestus are smitten by sturdy hammers, and tell him to still the blasts of fire until *Argo* pass by them. Then go to Aeolus too, Aeolus who rules the winds, children of the clear sky; and to him also tell my purpose so that he may make all winds cease under heaven and no breeze may ruffle the sea; yet let the breath of the west wind blow until the heroes have reached the Phaeacian isle of Alcinous."

So she spake, and straightway Iris leapt down from Olympus and cleft her way, with light wings outspread. And she plunged into the Aegean Sea, where is the dwelling of Nereus. And she came to Thetis first and, by the promptings of Hera, told her tale and roused her to go to the goddess. Next she came to Hephaestus, and quickly made him cease from the clang of his iron hammers; and the smoke-grimed bellows were stayed from their blast. And thirdly she came to Aeolus, the famous son of Hippotas. And when she had given her message to him also and rested her swift knees from her course, then Thetis leaving Nereus and her sisters had come from the sea to Olympus to the goddess Hera; and the goddess made her sit by her side and uttered her word:

"Hearken now, lady Thetis, to what I am eager to tell thee. Thou knowest how honoured in my heart is the hero, Aeson's son, and the others that have helped him in the contest, and how I saved them when they passed between the Wandering rocks[31] where roar terrible storms of fire and the waves foam round the rugged reefs. And now past the mighty rock of Scylla and Charybdis horribly belching, a course awaits them. But thee indeed from thy infancy did I tend with my own hands and love beyond all others that dwell in the salt sea because thou didst

---

31. The *Symplegades* are referred to, where help was given by Athena, not by Hera. It is strange that no mention is made of the *Planctae*, properly so called, past which they are soon to be helped. Perhaps some lines have fallen out.

refuse to share the couch of Zeus for all his desire. For to him such deeds are ever dear, to embrace either goddesses or mortal women. But in reverence for me and with fear in thy heart thou didst shrink from his love; and he then swore a mighty oath that thou shouldst never be called the bride of an immortal god. Yet he ceased not from spying thee against thy will, until reverend Themis declared to him the whole truth, how that it was thy fate to bear a son mightier than his sire; wherefore he gave thee up, for all his desire, fearing lest another should be his match and rule the immortals, and in order that he might ever hold his own dominion. But I gave thee the best of the sons of earth to be thy husband, that thou mightest find a marriage dear to thy heart and bear children; and I summoned to the feast the gods, one and all. And with my own hand I raised the bridal torch, in return for the kindly honour thou didst pay me. But come, let me tell a tale that erreth not. When thy son shall come to the Elysian plain, he whom now in the home of Cheiron the Centaur water-nymphs are tending, though he still craves thy mother milk, it is fated that he be the husband of Medea, Aeetes' daughter; do thou aid thy daughter-in-law as a mother-in-law should, and aid Peleus himself. Why is thy wrath so steadfast? He was blinded by folly. For blindness comes even upon the gods. Surely at my behest I deem that Hephaestus will cease from kindling the fury of his flame, and that Aeolus, son of Hippotas, will check his swift rushing winds, all but the steady west wind, until they reach the havens of the Phaeacians; do thou devise a return without bane. The rocks and the tyrannous waves are my fear, they alone, and them thou canst foil with thy sisters' aid. And let them not fall in their helplessness into Charybdis lest she swallow them at one gulp, or approach the hideous lair of Scylla, Ausonian Scylla the deadly, whom night-wandering Hecate, who is called Crataeis,[32] bare to Phorcys, lest swooping upon them with her horrible jaws she destroy the chiefest of the heroes. But guide their ship in the course where there shall be still a hair's breadth escape from destruction."

Thus she spake, and Thetis answered with these words: "If the fury of the ravening flame and the stormy winds cease in very deed, surely will I promise boldly to save the ship, even though the waves bar the way, if only the west wind blows fresh and clear. But it is time to fare on a long and measureless path, in quest of my sisters who will aid me, and

---

32. i.e. the Mighty One.

to the spot where the ship's hawsers are fastened, that at early dawn the heroes may take thought to win their home-return."

She spake, and darting down from the sky fell amid the eddies of the dark blue sea; and she called aid her the rest of the Nereids, her own sisters; and they heard her and gathered together; and Thetis declared to them Hera's behests, and quickly sped them all on their way to the Ausonian sea. And herself, swifter than the flash of an eye or the hafts of the sun, when it rises upwards from a far-distant land, hastened swiftly through the sea, until she reached the Aeaean beach of the Tyrrhenian mainland. And the heroes she found by the ship taking their pastime, with quoits and shooting of arrows; and she drew near and just touched the hand of Aeacus' son Peleus, for he was her husband; nor could anyone see her clearly, but she appeared to his eyes alone, and thus addressed him:

"No longer now must ye stay sitting on the Tyrrhenian beach, but at dawn loosen the hawsers of your swift ship, in obedience to Hera, your helper. For at her behest the maiden daughters of Nereus have met together to draw your ship through the midst of the rocks which are called Planctae,[33] for that is your destined path. But do thou show my person to no one, when thou seest us come to meet thee, but keep it secret in thy mind, lest thou anger me still more than thou didst anger me before so recklessly."

She spake, and vanished into the depths of the sea; but sharp pain smote Peleus, for never before had he seen her come, since first she left her bridal chamber and bed in anger, on account of noble Achilles, then a babe. For she ever encompassed the child's mortal flesh in the night with the flame of fire; and day by day she anointed with ambrosia his tender frame, so that he might become immortal and that she might keep off from his body loathsome old age. But Peleus leapt up from his bed and saw his dear son gasping in the flame; and at the sight he uttered a terrible cry, fool that he was; and she heard it, and catching up the child threw him screaming to the ground, and herself like a breath of wind passed swiftly from the hall as a dream and leapt into the sea, exceeding wroth, and thereafter returned not again. Wherefore blank amazement fettered his soul; nevertheless he declared to his comrades all the bidding of Thetis. And they broke off in the midst and hurriedly ceased their contests, and prepared their meal and earth-strewn beds, whereon after supper they slept through the night as aforetime.

---

33. i.e. the Wanderers.

Now when dawn the light-bringer was touching the edge of heaven, then at the coming of the swift west wind they went to their thwarts from the land; and gladly did they draw up the anchors from the deep and made the tackling ready in due order; and above spread the sail, stretching it taut with the sheets from the yard-arm. And a fresh breeze wafted the ship on. And soon they saw a fair island, Anthemoessa, where the clear-voiced Sirens, daughters of Achelous, used to beguile with their sweet songs whoever cast anchor there, and then destroy him. Them lovely Terpsichore, one of the Muses, bare, united with Achelous; and once they tended Demeter's noble daughter still unwed, and sang to her in chorus; and at that time they were fashioned in part like birds and in part like maidens to behold. And ever on the watch from their place of prospect with its fair haven, often from many had they taken away their sweet return, consuming them with wasting desire; and suddenly to the heroes, too, they sent forth from their lips a lily-like voice. And they were already about to cast from the ship the hawsers to the shore, had not Thracian Orpheus, son of Oeagrus, stringing in his hands his Bistonian lyre, rung forth the hasty snatch of a rippling melody so that their ears might be filled with the sound of his twanging; and the lyre overcame the maidens' voice. And the west wind and the sounding wave rushing astern bore the ship on; and the Sirens kept uttering their ceaseless song. But even so the goodly son of Teleon alone of the comrades leapt before them all from the polished bench into the sea, even Butes, his soul melted by the clear ringing voice of the Sirens; and he swam through the dark surge to mount the beach, poor wretch. Quickly would they have robbed him of his return then and there, but the goddess that rules Eryx, Cypris, in pity snatched him away, while yet in the eddies, and graciously meeting him saved him to dwell on the Lilybean height. And the heroes, seized by anguish, left the Sirens, but other perils still worse, destructive to ships, awaited them in the meeting-place of the seas.

For on one side appeared the smooth rock of Scylla; on the other Charybdis ceaselessly spouted and roared; in another part the Wandering rocks were booming beneath the mighty surge, where before the burning flame spurted forth from the top of the crags, above the rock glowing with fire, and the air was misty with smoke, nor could you have seen the sun's light. Then, though Hephaestus had ceased from his toils, the sea was still sending up a warm vapour. Hereupon on this side and on that the daughters of Nereus met them; and behind, lady Thetis set her hand to the rudder-blade, to guide them amid the Wandering rocks. And as when in fair weather herds of dolphins come up from the depths and sport in circles round a ship as it speeds along, now seen in front, now behind, now again at the side—and delight comes to the sailors; so the Nereids darted upward and circled in their ranks round the ship *Argo*, while Thetis guided its course. And when they were about to touch the Wandering rocks, straightway they raised the edge of their garments over their snow-white knees, and aloft on the very rocks and where the waves broke, they hurried along on this side and on that apart from one another. And the ship was raised aloft as the current smote her, and all around the furious wave mounting up broke over the rocks, which at one time touched the sky like towering crags, at another, down in the depths, were fixed fast at the bottom of the sea and the fierce waves poured over them in floods. And the Nereids, even as maidens near some sandy beach roll their garments up to their waists out of their way and sport with a shapely-rounded ball; then they catch it one from another and send it high into the air; and it never touches the ground; so they in turn one from another sent the ship through the air over the waves, as it sped on ever away from the rocks; and round them the water spouted and foamed. And lord Hephaestus himself standing on the summit of a smooth rock and resting his massy shoulder on the handle of his hammer, beheld them, and the spouse of Zeus beheld them as she stood above the gleaming heaven; and she threw her arms round Athena, such fear seized her as she gazed. And as long as the space of a day is lengthened out in springtime, so long a time did they toil, heaving the ship between the loud-echoing rocks; then again the heroes caught the wind and sped onward; and swiftly they passed the mead of Thrinacia, where the kine of Helios fed. There the nymphs, like sea-mews, plunged beneath the depths, when they had fulfilled the behests of the spouse of Zeus. And at the same time the bleating of sheep came to the heroes through the mist and the lowing of kine, near at hand, smote their ears. And over the dewy leas Phaëthusa, the youngest of the daughters of Helios, tended the sheep, bearing in her hand a silver crook; while Lampetia, herding the kine, wielded a staff of glowing orichalcum[34] as she followed. These kine the heroes saw feeding by the river's stream, over the plain and the water-meadow; not one of them was dark in hue but all were white as milk and glorying in their horns

---

34. A fabulous metal, resembling gold in appearance.

of gold. So they passed them by in the day-time, and when night came on they were cleaving a great sea-gulf, rejoicing, until again early rising dawn threw light upon their course.

Fronting the Ionian gulf there lies an island in the Ceraunian sea, rich in soil, with a harbour on both sides, beneath which lies the sickle, as legend saith—grant me grace, O Muses, not willingly do I tell this tale of olden days—wherewith Cronos pitilessly mutilated his father; but others call it the reaping-hook of Demeter, goddess of the nether world. For Demeter once dwelt in that island, and taught the Titans to reap the ears of corn, all for the love of Macris. Whence it is called Drepane,[35] the sacred nurse of the Phaeacians; and thus the Phaeacians themselves are by birth of the blood of Uranus. To them came *Argo*, held fast by many toils, borne by the breezes from the Thrinacian sea; and Alcinous and his people with kindly sacrifice gladly welcomed their coming; and over them all the city made merry; thou wouldst say they were rejoicing over their own sons. And the heroes themselves strode in gladness through the throng, even as though they had set foot in the heart of Haemonia; but soon were they to arm and raise the battle-cry; so near to them appeared a boundless host of Colchians, who had passed through the mouth of Pontus and between the Cyanean rocks in search of the chieftains. They desired forthwith to carry off Medea to her father's house apart from the rest, or else they threatened with fierce cruelty to raise the dread war-cry both then and thereafter on the coming of Aeetes. But lordly Alcinous checked them amid their eagerness for war. For he longed to allay the lawless strife between both sides without the clash of battle. And the maiden in deadly fear often implored the comrades of Aeson's son, and often with her hands touched the knees of Arete, the bride of Alcinous:

"I beseech thee, O queen, be gracious and deliver me not to the Colchians to be borne to my father, if thou thyself too art one of the race of mortals, whose heart rushes swiftly to ruin from light transgressions. For my firm sense forsook me—it was not for wantonness. Be witness the sacred light of Helios, be witness the rites of the maiden that wanders by night, daughter of Perses. Not willingly did I haste from my home with men of an alien race but a horrible fear wrought on me to bethink me of flight when I sinned; other device was there none. Still my maiden's girdle remains, as in the halls of my father, unstained,

35. i.e. the Sickle-island.

untouched. Pity me, lady, and turn thy lord to mercy; and may the immortals grant thee a perfect life, and joy, and children, and the glory of a city unravaged!"

Thus did she implore Arete, shedding tears, and thus each of the chieftains in turn:

"On your account, ye men of peerless might, and on account of my toils in your ventures am I sorely afflicted; even I, by whose help ye yoked the bulls, and reaped the deadly harvest of the earthborn men; even I, through whom on your homeward path ye shall bear to Haemonia the golden fleece. Lo, here am I, who have lost my country and my parents, who have lost my home and all the delights of life; to you have I restored your country and your homes; with eyes of gladness ye will see again your parents; but from me a heavy-handed god has reft all joy; and with strangers I wander, an accursed thing. Fear your covenant and your oaths, fear the Fury that avenges suppliants and the retribution of heaven, if I fall into Aeetes' hands and am slain with grievous outrage. To no shrines, no tower of defence, no other refuge do I pay heed, but/only to you. Hard and pitiless in your cruelty! No reverence have ye for me in your heart though ye see me helpless, stretching my hands towards the knees of a stranger queen; yet, when ye longed to seize the fleece, would have met all the Colchians face to face and haughty Aeetes himself; but now ye have forgotten your courage, now that they are all alone and cut off."

Thus she spake, beseeching; and to whomsoever she bowed in prayer, that man tried to give her heart and to check her anguish. And in their hands they shook their sharp pointed spears, and drew the swords from their sheaths; and they swore they would not hold back from giving succour, if she should meet with an unrighteous judgement. And the host were all wearied and Night came on them, Night that puts to rest the works of men, and lulled all the earth to sleep; but to the maid no sleep brought rest, but in her bosom her heart was wrung with anguish. Even as when a toiling woman turns her spindle through the night, and round her moan her orphan children, for she is a widow, and down her cheeks fall the tears, as she bethinks her how dreary a lot hath seized her; so Medea's cheeks were wet; and her heart within her was in agony, pierced with sharp pain.

Now within the palace in the city, as aforetime, lay lordly Alcinous and Arete, the revered wife of Alcinous, and on their couch through the night they were devising plans about the maiden; and him, as her wedded husband, the wife addressed with loving words:

"Yea, my friend, come, save the woe-stricken maid from the Colchians and show grace to the Minyae. *Argos* is near our isle and the men of Haemonia; but Aeetes dwells not near, nor do we know of Aeetes one whit: we hear but his name; but this maiden of dread suffering hath broken my heart by her prayers. O king, give her not up to the Colchians to be borne back to her father's home. She was distraught when first she gave him the drugs to charm the oxen; and next, to cure one ill by another, as in our sinning we do often, she fled from her haughty sire's heavy wrath. But Jason, as I hear, is bound to her by mighty oaths that he will make her his wedded wife within his halls. Wherefore, my friend, make not, of thy will, Aeson's son to be forsworn, nor let the father, if thou canst help, work with angry heart some intolerable mischief on his child. For fathers are all too jealous against their children; what wrong did Nycteus devise against Antiope, fair of face! What woes did Danae endure on the wide sea through her sire's mad rage! Of late, and not far away, Echetus in wanton cruelty thrust spikes of bronze in his daughter's eyes; and by a grievous fate is she wasting away, grinding grains of bronze in a dungeon's gloom."

Thus she spake, beseeching; and by his wife's words his heart was softened, and thus he spake:

"Arete, with arms I could drive forth the Colchians, showing grace to the heroes for the maiden's sake. But I fear to set at nought the righteous judgment of Zeus. Nor is it well to take no thought of Aeetes, as thou sayest: for none is more lordly than Aeetes. And, if he willed, he might bring war upon Hellas, though he dwell afar. Wherefore it is right for me to deliver the judgement that in all men's eyes shall be best; and I will not hide it from thee. If she be yet a maid I decree that they carry her back to her father; but if she shares a husband's bed, I will not separate her from her lord; nor, if she bear a child beneath her breast, will I give it up to an enemy."

Thus he spake, and at once sleep laid him to rest. And she stored up in her heart the word of wisdom, and straightway rose from her couch and went through the palace; and her handmaids came hasting together, eagerly tending their mistress. But quietly she summoned her herald and addressed him, in her prudence urging Aeson's son to wed the maiden, and not to implore Alcinous; for he himself, she said, will decree to the Colchians that if she is still a maid he will deliver her up to be borne to her father's house, but that if she shares a husband's bed he will not sever her from wedded love.

Thus she spake, and quickly from the hall his feet bore him, that he might declare to Jason the fair-omened speech of Arete and the counsel of god-fearing Alcinous. And he found the heroes watching in full armour in the haven of Hyllus, near the city; and out he spake the whole message; and each hero's heart rejoiced; for the word that he spake was welcome.

And straightway they mingled a bowl to the blessed ones, as is right, and reverently led sheep to the altar, and for that very night prepared for the maiden the bridal couch in the sacred cave, where once dwelt Macris, the daughter of Aristaeus, lord of honey, who discovered the works of bees and the fatness of the olive, the fruit of labour. She it was that first received in her bosom the Nysean son of Zeus in Abantian Euboea, and with honey moistened his parched lips when Hermes bore him out of the flame. And Hera beheld it, and in wrath drove her from the whole island. And she accordingly came to dwell far off, in the sacred cave of the Phaeacians, and granted boundless wealth to the inhabitants. There at that time did they spread a mighty couch; and thereon they laid the glittering fleece of gold, that so the marriage might be made honoured and the theme of song. And for them nymphs gathered flowers of varied hue and bore them thither in their white bosoms; and a splendour as of flame played round them all, such a light gleamed from the golden tufts. And in their eyes it kindled a sweet longing; yet for all her desire, awe withheld each one from laying her hand thereon. Some were called daughters of the river Aegaeus; others dwelt round the crests of the Meliteian mount; and others were woodland nymphs from the plains. For Hera herself, the spouse of Zeus, had sent them to do honour to Jason. That cave is to this day called the sacred cave of Medea, where they spread the fine and fragrant linen and brought these two together. And the heroes in their hands wielded their spears for war, lest first a host of foes should burst upon them for battle unawares, and, their heads enwreathed with leafy sprays, all in harmony, while Orpheus' harp rang clear, sang the marriage song at the entrance to the bridal chamber. Yet not in the house of Alcinous was the hero, Aeson's son, minded to complete his marriage, but in his father's hall when he had returned home to Iolcus; and such was the mind of Medea herself; but necessity led them to wed at this time. For never in truth do we tribes of woe-stricken mortals tread the path of delight with sure foot; but still some bitter affliction keeps pace with our joy; Wherefore they too, though their souls were melted with sweet love, were held by fear, whether the sentence of Alcinous would be fulfilled.

Now dawn returning with her beams divine scattered the gloomy night through the sky; and the island beaches laughed out and the paths over the plains far off, drenched with dew, and there was a din in the streets; the people were astir throughout the city, and far away the Colchians were astir at the bounds of the isle of Macris. And straightway to them went Alcinous, by reason of his covenant, to declare his purpose concerning the maiden, and in his hand he held a golden staff, his staff of justice, whereby the people had righteous judgments meted out to them throughout the city. And with him in order due and arrayed in their harness of war went marching, band by band, the chiefs of the Phaeacians. And from the towers came forth the women in crowds to gaze upon the heroes; and the country folk came to meet them when they heard the news, for Hera had sent forth a true report. And one led the chosen ram of his flock, and another a heifer that had never toiled; and others set hard by jars of wine for mixing; and the smoke of sacrifice leapt up far away. And women bore fine linen, the fruit of much toil, as women will, and gifts of gold and varied ornaments as well, such as are brought to newly-wedded brides; and they marvelled when they saw the shapely forms and beauty of the gallant heroes, and among them the son of Oeagrus, oft beating the ground with gleaming sandal, to the time of his loud-ringing lyre and song. And all the nymphs together, whenever he recalled the marriage, uplifted the lovely bridal-chant; and at times again they sang alone as they circled in the dance, Hera, in thy honour; for it was thou that didst put it into the heart of Arete to proclaim the wise word of Alcinous. And as soon as he had uttered the decree of his righteous judgement, and the completion of the marriage had been proclaimed, he took care that thus it should abide fixed; and no deadly fear touched him nor Aeetes' grievous wrath, but he kept his judgement fast bound by unbroken oaths. So when the Colchians learnt that they were beseeching in vain and he bade them either observe his judgements or hold their ships away from his harbours and land, then they began to dread the threats of their own king and besought Alcinous to receive them as comrades; and there in the island long time they dwelt with the Phaeacians, until in the course of years, the Bacchiadae, a race sprung from Ephyra,[36] settled among them; and the Colchians

---

36. The old name of Corinth.

passed to an island opposite; and thence they were destined to reach the Ceraunian hills of the Abantes, and the Nestaeans and Oricum; but all this was fulfilled after long ages had passed. And still the altars which Medea built on the spot sacred to Apollo, god of shepherds, receive yearly sacrifices in honour of the Fates and the Nymphs. And when the Minyae departed many gifts of friendship did Alcinous bestow, and many Arete; moreover she gave Medea twelve Phaeacian handmaids from the palace, to bear her company. And on the seventh day they left Drepane; and at dawn came a fresh breeze from Zeus. And onward they sped borne along by the wind's breath. Howbeit not yet was it ordained for the heroes to set foot on Achaea, until they had toiled even in the furthest bounds of Libya.

Now had they left behind the gulf named after the Ambracians, now with sails wide spread the land of the Curetes, and next in order the narrow islands with the Echinades, and the land of Pelops was just descried; even then a baleful blast of the north wind seized them in mid-course and swept them towards the Libyan sea nine nights and as many days, until they came far within Syrtis, wherefrom is no return for ships, when they are once forced into that gulf. For on every hand are shoals, on every hand masses of seaweed from the depths; and over them the light foam of the wave washes without noise; and there is a stretch of sand to the dim horizon; and there moveth nothing that creeps or flies. Here accordingly the flood-tide—for this tide often retreats from the land and bursts back again over the beach coming on with a rush and roar—thrust them suddenly on to the innermost shore, and but little of the keel was left in the water. And they leapt forth from the ship, and sorrow seized them when they gazed on the mist and the levels of vast land stretching far like a mist and continuous into the distance; no spot for water, no path, no steading of herdsmen did they descry afar off, but all the scene was possessed by a dead calm. And thus did one hero, vexed in spirit, ask another:

"What land is this? Whither has the tempest hurled us? Would that, reckless of deadly fear, we had dared to rush on by that same path between the clashing rocks! Better were it to have overleapt the will of Zeus and perished in venturing some mighty deed. But now what should we do, held back by the winds to stay here, if ever so short a time? How desolate looms before us the edge of the limitless land!"

Thus one spake; and among them Ancaeus the helmsman, in despair at their evil case, spoke with grieving heart: "Verily we are undone by a terrible doom; there is no escape from ruin; we must suffer the cruellest woes, having fallen on this desolation, even though breezes should blow from the land; for, as I gaze far around, on every side do I behold a sea of shoals, and masses of water, fretted line upon line, run over the hoary sand. And miserably long ago would our sacred ship have been shattered far from the shore; but the tide itself bore her high on to the land from the deep sea. But now the tide rushes back to the sea, and only the foam, whereon no ship can sail, rolls round us, just covering the land. Wherefore I deem that all hope of our voyage and of our return is cut off. Let someone else show his skill; let him sit at the helm—the man that is eager for our deliverance. But Zeus has no will to fulfil our day of return after all our toils."

Thus he spake with tears, and all of them that had knowledge of ships agreed thereto; but the hearts of all grew numb, and pallor overspread their cheeks. And as, like lifeless spectres, men roam through a city awaiting the issue of war or of pestilence, or some mighty storm which overwhelms the countless labours of oxen, when the images of their own accord sweat and run down with blood, and bellowings are heard in temples, or when at mid-day the sun draws on night from heaven, and the stars shine clear through the mist; so at that time along the endless strand the chieftains wandered, groping their way. Then straightway dark evening came upon them; and piteously did they embrace each other and say farewell with tears, that they might, each one apart from his fellow, fall on the sand and die. And this way and that they went further to choose a resting-place; and they wrapped their heads in their cloaks and, fasting and unfed, lay down all that night and the day, awaiting a piteous death. But apart the maidens huddled together lamented beside the daughter of Aeetes. And as when, forsaken by their mother, unfledged birds that have fallen from a cleft in the rock chirp shrilly; or when by the banks of fair-flowing Pactolus, swans raise their song, and all around the dewy meadow echoes and the river's fair stream; so these maidens, laying in the dust their golden hair, all through the night wailed their piteous lament. And there all would have parted from life without a name and unknown to mortal men, those bravest of heroes, with their task unfulfilled; but as they pined in despair, the heroine-nymphs, warders of Libya, had pity on them, they who once found Athena, what time she leapt in gleaming armour from her father's head, and bathed her by Trito's waters. It was noon-tide and the fiercest rays of the sun were scorching Libya; they stood near

Aeson's son, and lightly drew the cloak from his head. And the hero cast down his eyes and looked aside, in reverence for the goddesses, and as he lay bewildered all alone they addressed him openly with gentle words:

"Ill-starred one, why art thou so smitten with despair? We know how ye went in quest of the golden fleece; we know each toil of yours, all the mighty deeds ye wrought in your wanderings over land and sea. We are the solitary ones, goddesses of the land, speaking with human voice, the heroines, Libya's warders and daughters. Up then; be not thus afflicted in thy misery, and rouse thy comrades. And when Amphitrite has straightway loosed Poseidon's swift-wheeled car, then do ye pay to your mother a recompense for all her travail when she bare you so long in her womb; and so ye may return to the divine land of Achaea."

Thus they spake, and with the voice vanished at once, where they stood. But Jason sat upon the earth as he gazed around, and thus cried:

"Be gracious, noble goddesses of the desert, yet the saying about our return I understand not clearly. Surely I will gather together my comrades and tell them, if haply we can find some token of our escape, for the counsel of many is better."

He spake, and leapt to his feet, and shouted afar to his comrades, all squalid with dust, like a lion when he roars through the woodland seeking his mate; and far off in the mountains the glens tremble at the thunder of his voice; and the oxen of the field and the herdsmen shudder with fear; yet to them Jason's voice was no whit terrible—the voice of a comrade calling to his friends. And with looks downcast they gathered near, and hard by where the ship lay he made them sit down in their grief and the women with them, and addressed them and told them everything:

"Listen, friends; as I lay in my grief, three goddesses girded with goat-skins from the neck downwards round the back and waist, like maidens, stood over my head nigh at hand; and they uncovered me, drawing my cloak away with light hand, and they bade me rise up myself and go and rouse you, and pay to our mother a bounteous recompense for all her travail when she bare us so long in her womb, when Amphitrite shall have loosed Poseidon's swift-wheeled car. But I cannot fully understand concerning this divine message. They said indeed that they were heroines, Libya's warders land daughters; and all the toils that we endured aforetime by land and sea, all these they declared that they knew full well. Then I saw them no more in their place, but a mist or cloud came between and hid them from my sight."

Thus he spake, and all marvelled as they heard. Then was wrought for the Minyae the strangest of portents. From the sea to the land leapt forth a monstrous horse, of vast size, with golden mane tossing round his neck; and quickly from his limbs he shook off abundant spray and started on his course, with feet like the wind. And at once Peleus rejoiced and spake among the throng of his comrades:

"I deem that Poseidon's car has even now been loosed by the hands of his dear wife, and I divine that our mother is none else than our ship herself; for surely she bare us in her womb and groans unceasingly with grievous travailing. But with unshaken strength and untiring shoulders will we lift her up and bear her within this country of sandy wastes, where yon swift-footed steed has sped before. For he will not plunge beneath the earth; and his hoof-prints, I ween, will point us to some bay above the sea."

Thus he spake, and the fit counsel pleased all. This is the tale the Muses told; and I sing obedient to the Pierides, and this report have I heard most truly; that ye, O mightiest far of the sons of kings, by your might and your valour over the desert sands of Libya raised high aloft on your shoulders the ship and all that ye brought therein, and bare her twelve days and nights alike. Yet who could tell the pain and grief which they endured in that toil? Surely they were of the blood of the immortals, such a task did they take on them, constrained by necessity. How forward and how far they bore her gladly to the waters of the Tritonian lake! How they strode in and set her down from their stalwart shoulders!

Then, like raging hounds, they rushed to search for a spring; for besides their suffering and anguish, a parching thirst lay upon them, and not in vain did they wander; but they came to the sacred plain where Ladon, the serpent of the land, till yesterday kept watch over the golden apples in the garden of Atlas; and all around the nymphs, the Hesperides, were busied, chanting their lovely song. But at that time, stricken by Heracles, he lay fallen by the trunk of the apple-tree; only the tip of his tail was still writhing; but from his head down his dark spine he lay lifeless; and where the arrows had left in his blood the bitter gall of the Lernaean hydra, flies withered and died over the festering wounds And close at hand the Hesperides, their white arms flung over their golden heads, lamented shrilly; and the heroes drew near suddenly; but the maidens, at their quick approach, at once became dust and earth where they stood. Orpheus marked the divine portent, and for his comrades addressed them in prayer: "O divine ones, fair and kind, be gracious, O queens, whether ye be numbered among the heavenly goddesses, or those beneath the earth, or be called the Solitary nymphs; come, O nymphs, sacred race of Oceanus, appear manifest to our longing eyes and show us some spring of water from the rock or some sacred flow gushing from the earth, goddesses, wherewith we may quench the thirst that burns us unceasingly. And if ever again we return in our voyaging to the Achaean land, then to you among the first of goddesses with willing hearts will we bring countless gifts, libations and banquets."

So he spake, beseeching them with plaintive voice; and they from their station near pitied their pain; and lo! first of all they caused grass to spring from the earth; and above the grass rose up tall shoots; and then flourishing saplings grew standing upright far above the earth. Hespere became a poplar and Eretheis an elm, and Aegle a willow's sacred trunk. And forth from these trees their forms looked out, as clear as they were before, a marvel exceeding great, and Aegle spake with gentle words answering their longing looks:

"Surely there has come hither a mighty succour to your toils, that most accursed man, who robbed our guardian serpent of life and plucked the golden apples of the goddesses and is gone; and has left bitter grief for us. For yesterday came a man most fell in wanton violence, most grim in form; and his eyes flashed beneath his scowling brow; a ruthless wretch; and he was clad in the skin of a monstrous lion of raw hide, untanned; and he bare a sturdy bow of olive, and a bow, wherewith he shot and killed this monster here. So he too came, as one traversing the land on foot, parched with thirst; and he rushed wildly through this spot, searching for water, but nowhere was he like to see it. Now here stood a rock near the Tritonian lake; and of his own device, or by the prompting of some god, he smote it below with his foot; and the water gushed out in full flow. And he, leaning both his hands and chest upon the ground, drank a huge draught from the rifted rock, until, stooping like a beast of the field, he had satisfied his mighty maw."

Thus she spake; and they gladly with joyful steps ran to the spot where Aegle had pointed out to them the spring, until they reached it. And as when earth-burrowing ants gather in swarms round a narrow cleft, or when flies lighting upon a tiny drop of sweet honey cluster round with insatiate eagerness; so at that time, huddled together, the Minyae thronged about the spring from the rock. And thus with wet lips one cried to another in his delight:

"Strange! In very truth Heracles, though far away, has saved his comrades, fordone with thirst. Would that we might find him on his way as we pass through the mainland!"

So they spake, and those who were ready for this work answered, and they separated this way and that, each starting to search. For by the night winds the footsteps had been effaced where the sand was stirred. The two sons of Boreas started up, trusting in their wings; and Euphemus, relying on his swift feet, and Lynceus to cast far his piercing eyes; and with them darted off Canthus, the fifth. He was urged on by the doom of the gods and his own courage, that he might learn for certain from Heracles where he had left Polyphemus, son of Eilatus; for he was minded to question him on every point concerning his comrade. But that hero had founded a glorious city among the Mysians, and, yearning for his home-return, had passed far over the mainland in search of *Argo*; and in time he reached the land of the Chalybes, who dwell near the sea; there it was that his fete subdued him. And to him a monument stands under a tall poplar, just facing the sea. But that day Lynceus thought he saw Heracles all alone, far off, over measureless land, as a man at the month's beginning sees, or thinks he sees, the moon through a bank of cloud. And he returned and told his comrades that no other searcher would find Heracles on his way, and they also came back, and swift-footed Euphemus and the twin sons of Thracian Boreas, after a vain toil.

But thee, Canthus, the fates of death seized in Libya. On pasturing flocks didst thou light; and there followed a shepherd who, in defence of his own sheep, while thou wert leading them off [37] to thy comrades in their need, slew thee by the cast of a stone; for he was no weakling, Caphaurus, the grandson of Lycoreian Phoebus and the chaste maiden Acacallis, whom once Minos drove from home to dwell in Libya, his own daughter, when she was bearing the gods' heavy load; and she bare to Phoebus a glorious son, whom they call Amphithemis and Garamas. And Amphithemis wedded a Tritonian nymph; and she bare to him Nasamon and strong Caphaurus, who on that day in defending his sheep slew Canthus. But he escaped not the chieftains' avenging hands, when they learned the deed he had done. And the Minyae, when they knew it, afterwards took up the corpse and buried it in the earth, mourning; and the sheep they took with them.

---

37. This seems to be the only possible translation, but the optative is quite anomalous. We should expect.

Thereupon on the same day a pitiless fate seized Mopsus too, son of Ampycus; and he escaped not a bitter doom by his prophesying; for there is no averting of death. Now there lay in the sand, avoiding the midday heat, a dread serpent, too sluggish of his own will to strike at an unwilling foe, nor yet would he dart full face at one that would shrink back. But into whatever of all living beings that life-giving earth sustains that serpent once injects his black venom, his path to Hades becomes not so much as a cubit's length, not even if Paeëon, if it is right for me to say this openly, should tend him, when its teeth have only grazed the skin. For when over Libya flew godlike Perseus Eurymedon—for by that name his mother called him—bearing to the king the Gorgon's head newly severed, all the drops of dark blood that fell to the earth, produced a brood of those serpents. Now Mopsus stepped on the end of its spine, setting thereon the sole of his left foot; and it writhed round in pain and bit and tore the flesh between the shin and the muscles. And Medea and her handmaids fled in terror; but Canthus bravely felt the bleeding wound; for no excessive pain harassed him. Poor wretch! Already a numbness that loosed his limbs was stealing beneath his skin, and a thick mist was spreading over his eyes. Straightway his heavy limbs sank helplessly to the ground and he grew cold; and his comrades and the hero, Aeson's son, gathered round, marvelling at the close-coming doom. Nor yet though dead might he lie beneath the sun even for a little space. For at once the poison began to rot his flesh within, and the hair decayed and fell from the skin. And quickly and in haste they dug a deep grave with mattocks of bronze; and they tore their hair, the heroes and the maidens, bewailing the dead man's piteous suffering; and when he had received due burial rites, thrice they marched round the tomb in full armour, and heaped above him a mound of earth.

But when they had gone aboard, as the south wind blew over the sea, and they were searching for a passage to go forth from the Tritonian lake, for long they had no device, but all the day were borne on aimlessly. And as a serpent goes writhing along his crooked path when the sun's fiercest rays scorch him; and with a hiss he turns his head to this side and that, and in his fury his eyes glow like sparks of fire, until he creeps to his lair through a cleft in the rock; so *Argo* seeking an outlet from the lake, a fairway for ships, wandered for a long time. Then straightway Orpheus bade them bring forth from the ship Apollo's massy tripod and offer it to the gods of the land as propitiation for their return. So they went forth and set Apollo's gift on the shore; then before them stood, in the form of a youth, far-swaying Triton, and he lifted a clod from the earth and offered it as a stranger's gift, and thus spake:

"Take it, friends, for no stranger's gift of great worth have I here by me now to place in the hands of those who beseech me. But if ye are searching for a passage through this sea, as often is the need of men passing through a strange land, I will declare it. For my sire Poseidon has made me to be well versed in this sea. And I rule the shore—if haply in your distant land you have ever heard of Eurypylus, born in Libya, the home of wild beasts."

Thus he spake, and readily Euphemus held out his hands towards the clod, and thus addressed him in reply:

"If haply, hero, thou knowest aught of Apis[38] and the sea of Minos, tell us truly, who ask it of you. For not of our will have we come hither, but by the stress of heavy storms have we touched the borders of this land, and have borne our ship aloft on our shoulders to the waters of this lake over the mainland, grievously burdened; and we know not where a passage shows itself for our course to the land of Pelops."

So he spake; and Triton stretched out his hand and showed afar the sea and the lake's deep mouth, and then addressed them: "That is the outlet to the sea, where the deep water lies unmoved and dark; on each side roll white breakers with shining crests; and the way between for your passage out is narrow. And that sea stretches away in mist to the divine land of Pelops beyond Crete; but hold to the right, when ye have entered the swell of the sea from the lake, and steer your course hugging the land, as long as it trends to the north; but when the coast bends, falling away in the other direction, then your course is safely laid for you if ye go straight forward from the projecting cape. But go in joy, and as for labour let there be no grieving that limbs in youthful vigour should still toil."

He spake with kindly counsel; and they at once went aboard, intent to come forth from the lake by the use of oars. And eagerly they sped on; meanwhile Triton took up the mighty tripod, and they saw him enter the lake; but thereafter did no one mark how he vanished so near them along with the tripod. But their hearts were cheered, for that one of the blessed had met them in friendly guise. And they bade Aeson's son offer to him the choicest of the sheep and when he had slain it

---

38. An old name of the Peloponnesus.

chant the hymn of praise. And straightway he chose in haste and raising the victim slew it over the stern, and prayed with these words:

"Thou god, who hast manifested thyself on the borders of this land, whether the daughters born of the sea call thee Triton, the great sea-marvel, or Phorcys, or Nereus, be gracious, and grant the return home dear to our hearts."

He spake, and cut the victim's throat over the water and cast it from the stern. And the god rose up from the depths in form such as he really was. And as when a man trains a swift steed for the broad race-course, and runs along, grasping the bushy mane, while the steed follows obeying his master, and rears his neck aloft in his pride, and the gleaming bit rings loud as he champs it in his jaws from side to side; so the god, seizing hollow *Argo*'s keel, guided her onward to the sea. And his body, from the crown of his head, round his back and waist as far as the belly, was wondrously like that of the blessed ones in form; but below his sides the tail of a sea monster lengthened far, forking to this side and that; and he smote the surface of the waves with the spines, which below parted into curving fins, like the horns of the new moon. And he guided *Argo* on until he sped her into the sea on her course; and quickly he plunged into the vast abyss; and the heroes shouted when they gazed with their eyes on that dread portent. There is the harbour of *Argo* and there are the signs of her stay, and altars to Poseidon and Triton; for during that day they tarried. But at dawn with sails outspread they sped on before the breath of the west wind, keeping the desert land on their right. And on the next morn they saw the headland and the recess of the sea, bending inward beyond the jutting headland. And straightway the west wind ceased, and there came the breeze of the clear south wind: and their hearts rejoiced at the sound it made. But when the sun sank and the star returned that bids the shepherd fold, which brings rest to wearied ploughmen, at that time the wind died down in the dark night; so they furled the sails and lowered the tall mast and vigorously plied their polished oars all night and through the day, and again when the next night came on. And rugged Carpathus far away welcomed them; and thence they were to cross to Crete, which rises in the sea above other islands.

And Talos, the man of bronze, as he broke off rocks from the hard cliff, stayed them from fastening hawsers to the shore, when they came to the road-stead of Dicte's haven. He was of the stock of bronze, of the men sprung from ash-trees, the last left among the sons of the gods; and the son of Cronos gave him to Europa to be the warder of Crete and to stride round the island thrice a day with his feet of bronze. Now in all the rest of his body and limbs was he fashioned of bronze and invulnerable; but beneath the sinew by his ankle was a blood-red vein; and this, with its issues of life and death, was covered by a thin skin. So the heroes, though outworn with toil, quickly backed their ship from the land in sore dismay. And now far from Crete would they have been borne in wretched plight, distressed both by thirst and pain, had not Medea addressed them as they turned away:

"Hearken to me. For I deem that I alone can subdue for you that man, whoever he be, even though his frame be of bronze throughout, unless his life too is everlasting. But be ready to keep your ship here beyond the cast of his stones, till he yield the victory to me."

Thus she spake; and they drew the ship out of range, resting on their oars, waiting to see what plan unlooked for she would bring to pass; and she, holding the fold of her purple robe over her cheeks on each side, mounted on the deck; and Aeson's son took her hand in his and guided her way along the thwarts. And with songs did she propitiate and invoke the Death-spirits, devourers of life, the swift hounds of Hades, who, hovering through all the air, swoop down on the living. Kneeling in supplication, thrice she called on them with songs, and thrice with prayers; and, shaping her soul to mischief, with her hostile glance she bewitched the eyes of Talos, the man of bronze; and her teeth gnashed bitter wrath against him, and she sent forth baneful phantoms in the frenzy of her rage.

Father Zeus, surely great wonder rises in my mind, seeing that dire destruction meets us not from disease and wounds alone, but lo! even from afar, may be, it tortures us! So Talos, for all his frame of bronze, yielded the victory to the might of Medea the sorceress. And as he was heaving massy rocks to stay them from reaching the haven, he grazed his ankle on a pointed crag; and the ichor gushed forth like melted lead; and not long thereafter did he stand towering on the jutting cliff. But even as some huge pine, high up on the mountains, which woodmen have left half hewn through by their sharp axes when they returned from the forest—at first it shivers in the wind by night, then at last snaps at the stump and crashes down; so Talos for a while stood on his tireless feet, swaying to and fro, then at last, all strengthless, fell with a mighty thud. For that night there in Crete the heroes lay; then, just as dawn was growing bright, they built a shrine to Minoan Athena, and drew water and went aboard, so that first of all they might by rowing pass beyond Salmone's height.

But straightway as they sped over the wide Cretan sea night scared them, that night which they name the Pall of Darkness; the stars pierced not that fatal night nor the beams of the moon, but black chaos descended from heaven, or haply some other darkness came, rising from the nethermost depths. And the heroes, whether they drifted in Hades or on the waters, knew not one whit; but they committed their return to the sea in helpless doubt whither it was bearing them. But Jason raised his hands and cried to Phoebus with mighty voice, calling on him to save them; and the tears ran down in his distress; and often did he promise to bring countless offerings to Pytho, to Amyclae, and to Ortygia. And quickly, O son of Leto, swift to hear, didst thou come down from heaven to the Melantian rocks, which lie there in the sea. Then darting upon one of the twin peaks, thou raisedst aloft in thy right hand thy golden bow; and the bow flashed a dazzling gleam all round. And to their sight appeared a small island of the Sporades, over against the tiny isle Hippuris, and there they cast anchor and stayed; and straightway dawn arose and gave them light; and they made for Apollo a glorious abode in a shady wood, and a shady altar, calling on Phoebus the "Gleamer," because of the gleam far-seen; and that bare island they called Anaphe,[39] for that Phoebus had revealed it to men sore bewildered. And they sacrificed all that men could provide for sacrifice on a desolate strand; wherefore when Medea's Phaeacian handmaids saw them pouring water for libations on the burning brands, they could no longer restrain laughter within their bosoms, for that ever they had seen oxen in plenty slain in the halls of Alcinous. And the heroes delighted in the jest and attacked them with taunting words; and merry railing and contention flung to and fro were kindled among them. And from that sport of the heroes such scoffs do the women fling at the men in that island whenever they propitiate with sacrifices Apollo the gleaming god, the warder of Anaphe.

But when they had loosed the hawsers thence in fair weather, then Euphemus bethought him of a dream of the night, reverencing the glorious son of Maia. For it seemed to him that the god-given clod of earth held in his palm close to his breast was being suckled by white

---

39. i.e. the isle of Revealing.

streams of milk, and that from it, little though it was, grew a woman like a virgin; and he, overcome by strong desire, lay with her in love's embrace; and united with her he pitied her, as though she were a maiden whom he was feeding with his own milk; but she comforted him with gentle words:

"Daughter of Triton am I, dear friend, and nurse of thy children, no maiden; Triton and Libya are my parents. But restore me to the daughters of Nereus to dwell in the sea near Anaphe; I shall return again to the light of the sun, to prepare a home for thy descendants."

Of this he stored in his heart the memory, and declared it to Aeson's son; and Jason pondered a prophecy of the Far-Darter and lifted up his voice and said:

"My friend, great and glorious renown has fallen to thy lot. For of this clod when thou hast cast it into the sea, the gods will make an island, where thy children's children shall dwell; for Triton gave this to thee as a stranger's gift from the Libyan mainland. None other of the immortals it was than he that gave thee this when he met thee."

Thus he spake; and Euphemus made not vain the answer of Aeson's son; but, cheered by the prophecy, he cast the clod into the depths. Therefrom rose up an island, Calliste, sacred nurse of the sons of Euphemus, who in former days dwelt in Sintian Lemnos, and from Lemnos were driven forth by Tyrrhenians and came to Sparta as suppliants; and when they left Sparta, Theras, the goodly son of Autesion, brought them to the island Calliste, and from himself he gave it the name of Thera. But this befell after the days of Euphemus.

And thence they steadily left behind long leagues of sea and stayed on the beach of Aegina; and at once they contended in innocent strife about the fetching of water, who first should draw it and reach the ship. For both their need and the ceaseless breeze urged them on. There even to this day do the youths of the Myrmidons take up on their shoulders full-brimming jars, and with swift feet strive for victory in the race.

Be gracious, race of blessed chieftains! And may these songs year after year be sweeter to sing among men. For now have I come to the glorious end of your toils; for no adventure befell you as ye came home from Aegina, and no tempest of winds opposed you; but quietly did ye skirt the Cecropian land and Aulis inside of Euboea and the Opuntian cities of the Locrians, and gladly did ye step forth upon the beach of Pagasae.

A Note About the Author

Apollonius of Rhodes (third century BCE) was a Greek poet and scholar who studied under Callimachus at the Library of Alexandria. Historians claim it was there that his greatest work, *The Voyage of the Argo* or *The Argonautica*, was written but ultimately rejected by his peers. Apollonius would flee to Rhodes to revise the epic and return to great acclaim. Some report he was appointed chief librarian but eventually left the city to spend his final years on the island of Rhodes.

A Note from the Publisher

Spanning many genres, from non-fiction essays to literature classics to children's books and lyric poetry, Mint Edition books showcase the master works of our time in a modern new package. The text is freshly typeset, is clean and easy to read, and features a new note about the author in each volume. Many books also include exclusive new introductory material. Every book boasts a striking new cover, which makes it as appropriate for collecting as it is for gift giving. Mint Edition books are only printed when a reader orders them, so natural resources are not wasted. We're proud that our books are never manufactured in excess and exist only in the exact quantity they need to be read and enjoyed.

bookfinity™

Discover more of your favorite classics with Bookfinity™.

- Track your reading with custom book lists.
- Get great book recommendations for your personalized Reader Type.
- Add reviews for your favorite books.
- AND MUCH MORE!

Visit **bookfinity.com** and take the fun Reader Type quiz to get started.

Enjoy our classic and modern companion pairings!

Classic & Modern